THE WHOLE BEAUTIFUL WORLD

The Whole Beautiful World

Stories

MELISSA KUIPERS

BRINDLE
& GLASS

Brindle & Glass
An imprint of TouchWood Editions
Brindleandglass.com

This book is a work of fiction. Names, characters, places, and incidents are either products of the author's imagination or are used fictitiously. Any resemblance to actual events or locales or persons, living or dead, is entirely coincidental.

Edited by Colin Thomas
Copy edit by Kate Kennedy
Proofread by Cailey Cavallin
Cover design by Tree Abraham
Interior design by Pete Kohut

LIBRARY AND ARCHIVES CANADA CATALOGUING IN PUBLICATION
Kuipers, Melissa, author
The whole beautiful world : stories / Melissa Kuipers.

Issued also in electronic formats.
ISBN 978-1-927366-62-2 (softcover)

I. Title.

PS8621.U39W46 2017   C813'.6   C2017-903030-2

We acknowledge the financial support of the Government of Canada through the Canada Book Fund and the Canada Council for the Arts, and of the province of British Columbia through the British Columbia Arts Council and the Book Publishing Tax Credit.

The interior pages of this book have been printed on 100% post-consumer recycled paper, processed chlorine free, and printed with vegetable-based inks.

PRINTED IN CANADA AT FRIESENS

17 18 19 20 21   5 4 3 2 1

To Dad

CONTENTS

MOURNING WREATH

LIONEL CRANE WAS AS QUIET as they come. He was homeschooled for the first thirteen years of his life, and then transferred into our Grade 7 class when his mother decided she had nothing left to teach him. He could have gone right into high school, but the principal advised he stay with people his own age. He had a much smaller sense of personal space than the rest of us. He didn't stare at your chest when he talked to you, but he didn't look into your eyes either—always into your mouth, as if he were looking for some secret hanging from the end of your uvula.

The only thing that got Lionel a little respect was the fact that he was the tallest in the class and had already completed a voice change without any dips or squeaks. No one bothered him. He kept to himself mostly, and no one really knew where he went at lunchtime.

Just before Thanksgiving, the Grade 7s and 8s had a talent show. A bunch of the girls lip-synched Britney Spears songs, and some guys did an air band version of "Superman's Dead," and the rest of us were just glad to get out of class. Then Lionel came out of the wings in denim tights and a blue tank top. A teacher turned off the house-lights. Lionel stood in the middle of the stage, eyes glued to the floor, and then rose up on his bare toes, lifted his arms and performed the first contemporary dance routine we had ever seen. He danced to a slow romantic pop song that every boy in the class had put on the mixed CD he made for his girlfriend that year, a song sung with a smoky, questioning voice. He spun his skinny body around the stage with muscles I didn't think a thirteen-year-old could have. He flung his fluid legs above his head with a grace and confidence I didn't think possible for anyone our age. The girl sitting beside me said to me or the universe, "I'm going to make my boyfriend learn to do that."

That was when Lionel Crane and I became friends—not because he had earned popularity points, but because the tenderness of his motions showed me that he had something worth sharing. I made it my job to tell off every pimple-faced boy who dared to say Lionel was gay. I even flicked my eraser at Jonah MacKenzie's Adam's apple and told him he was just jealous when he asked Lionel if he was a fag. That day Lionel and I walked home from school together. We kept the tradition for the rest of the year.

His mother had been a ballerina—not a pretty one, but still a successful one. Mrs. Crane had met our town's optometrist, Lionel's father, while he was finishing his degree in Calgary. She was ten years older than him, and much older than most mothers of kids my age, but I only knew this because Lionel told me her age in secret once. He told me in exchange for my secret that our dog was half pit bull, but we didn't want to keep him in a muzzle all the time. He could have told me she was twenty-four or fifty and I would have believed him. The only thing that gave her age away were the thick strands of white hair running through her dark bun. She refused to dye them out the way most mothers did.

There were two things about Lionel's mother that fascinated me: she wore black painted-on eyeliner that met in a perfect narrow V at the corners of her eyes, and her legs, which were bare even in the dead of winter, were pure white and veinless. I thought all mothers had spider and varicose veins, that they appeared automatically when your blood pumped into someone else for nine months.

Since she had so much free time now that Lionel was in school, she rented the upstairs of the Legion one evening a week and started Talbot's first dance class. The impact of Lionel's performance was obvious when she ended up with a hundred kids who had spent the holidays twirling all over their families' living rooms until their parents relented. I didn't take lessons because my parents couldn't afford it, but, in the Cranes' basement with its walls lined in mirrors, Lionel would teach me how to stand in ballet shoes and spin without getting dizzy. He would improvise for me and then ask me to try.

"You know I can't dance," I'd say.

"Because you won't try," he'd say, smiling. He'd grab my hands and pull me into a crazy jitterbug, scrunching up his face with his tongue hanging out as if the movements took effort, as if they didn't flow naturally from somewhere deep and unreachable. I'd laugh and pull away, plunging my fists into my hoodie pouch. I'd curl up into one of the green faux-fur beanbag chairs with pink centres, and he'd collapse dramatically into the other. He told me once they looked like boobs. "Boys think everything looks like boobs," I said. I stood up and dropped my beanbag on him, then jumped on it.

I'd go home, close the curtains, blare Alanis Morissette and try to free my scraggly limbs to flow like his. Next time, I told myself, I would dance with him. I would be freer and less uptight and I'd be able to laugh at myself. But I'd catch a glimpse of myself in the mirror and my hands would fall at my sides. The next time we'd hang out I'd watch him again in awe and would never let him know how awkward I really was.

The summer between Grade 7 and 8 I helped my mom clean houses, while Lionel went with his mother to Vancouver where she had been cast as the mother in *Giselle*, and his father stayed home to check people's eyes.

Lionel and I thought Mom would seem more professional if we gave her business a name. Lionel came up with Keeping Kleen. I bought a khaki utility dress from the Goodwill and he took a Sharpie and drew a little feather duster on the breast pocket with two calligraphy Ks under it. The duster looked more like a mushroom and I told him that.

We sent each other postcards we made from cereal boxes. It became a game in testing Canada Post. One day he unravelled an entire roll of masking tape and wrote a message the whole length of it, then rolled it back up still in one continuous piece. Along the inside circle of cardboard he wrote, "All the tape in the world can't contain our love." He wrote my address along the outer layer and used four stamps for good measure. I never got it. He told me about it when he got home, and we laughed and I loved that it was worth all that effort to create something I might never see.

When he came back from out West halfway through September, it was clear something was different. His mother had spent the summer sleeping longer and longer, he told me, till she was going to sleep at eleven after the show, and waking up at noon the next day. Her performances were becoming more and more sloppy, and he had worried they would replace her permanently with the understudy. I wondered why he hadn't said anything about it in his postcards to me, and was glad he hadn't. He didn't bring it up again until October when she broke a hundred little hearts by cancelling her class for that term. Lionel got his father to pull him out of Grade 8 and register him as homeschooled so he could stay with his mom. It didn't take much convincing since he was way ahead of the rest of the class anyway.

Lionel's mother started covering her legs with long broom skirts when she started using a wheelchair. She lost the defining black lines around her eyes when she no longer had the strength to lift her arms for longer than a few seconds. Lionel kept updating me about the stages of her body breaking down, how her voice was changing, how she would soon need a machine to help her breathe. She had told him she didn't want to drag this dying thing out. She wanted to go gracefully, smoothly, and if she shut down she didn't want anyone reviving her.

I was okay with the way he was changing. I could handle him being sad all the time. But I couldn't stand myself for never knowing what to say. I would sit there in silence while he told me he had to cut her long, thick hair because she couldn't lift her arms to brush it, because she felt the weight of it too heavy along the back of her neck. I sat there willing myself to put my arm around his shoulder, but I'd freeze in fear. I'd try to moisten my stiff mouth to say something thoughtful and I'd just end up making nervous gulping sounds. I couldn't get myself to cry with him when he cried. I'd try to force the tears, try to imagine how I would feel if my mom died, but all I could do was sit there sweating, afraid to hold his hand because mine was so clammy.

I finally stopped visiting after the day Lionel and I sat at the kitchen counter playing Uno while Mrs. Crane sat nearby in her wheelchair. Her head was propped up with a foam neckpiece. Her new bob splayed out crazily around it. I skipped Lionel for the third time in a row and he swore. She started to snicker, then laugh. Her voice had started becoming nasally as her throat muscles began to relax. She laughed and laughed and I started laughing too. I laughed with her for a few seconds until I turned and saw that her eyes looked scared. Lionel had told me that sometimes that happened, that she cried or laughed for no reason. But he told me too many things about how her body was betraying her for me to keep track of it all. I kept laughing with her, looking into her scared eyes, my heart thudding. I couldn't look at him. I saw the bright colours of the cards droop in his hands as they went limp on the table. I could see his hand reaching out to touch my arm. I stood up before he could reach me. I was still laughing as I ran to the washroom and sat on the toilet and cried until I could hear her laughter trickle away.

After that I started going with Mom to work more often. I tried to fill my weekends with cleaning, told her I was saving up so I could buy a bike to get to school. I stopped wearing my khaki dress to work—I was outgrowing it anyway. He called twice for me, and then stopped trying. It made sense to me. He must have understood I wasn't the right person to talk to.

It went on like that for a couple months, me working a couple nights a week with Mom, doing some cleaning gigs with her on the weekend. I mostly liked it, seeing the kinds of crap people had, learning the different kinds of dust that accumulates in different kinds of houses, discovering the corners no one seems to care about. I loved finding a closet or basement full of cobwebs, standing on a stool with a broomstick and waving the handle around just below the ceiling till the webs wrapped in a fluffy cocoon of filth around the end of it.

Then one Saturday while I was staring at my finger-nails as we drove to work, Mom pulled the car into the Cranes' driveway.

"Mom, this is Lionel's house!"

"Oh, honey, I'm sorry—I didn't even make the con-nection."

"Drive me back home, please." I saw the curtain move in the front bay window, and Lionel's face flashed there for a second.

"I don't think I can very well do that now." I knew she was right. It would look awful if we left now that we'd been seen. "Besides, it'll make me late."

I slunk down into my seat. "I can't go in there."

"I think you can be a big girl about this. I don't see any problem—friends grow apart. You're here to work, anyway, not to socialize."

My heart was thudding as I reached into the trunk and lifted the bucket of cleaning supplies. The wooden porch made its familiar warm thudding sound as we walked up the steps.

Mr. Crane was sitting on a stool in the kitchen, in the same spot where I had had my fit. "Heidi, nice to see you again," he said. He smiled like he wanted to mean it.

"Lucille's resting in the other room, and Lionel's reading to her," he said.

"We'll make sure not to bother them," Mom said.

"Oh, no—I'm sure you won't be a bother," he said, his voice trailing at the end. "No bother at all." It was as if he had forgotten what the words meant. He left to do some work in the office. Mom sent me to work on the basement. I figured I'd have to go through an entire bottle of Windex to get the dust-speckled mirrors sparkling.

My heart slowed as I stood in the middle of the familiar mirror-covered room—the bureau and bankers boxes in one corner, the fuzzy green beanbag chairs with pink centres on the foam mats on the floor. I picked up one of the green blobs with both hands and threw it against a mirror. The mirror wiggled a bit and the tiny Styrofoam balls in the chair made a hushing sound as it slid down the wall. I didn't feel like staring at myself for an hour, so I started dusting the bureau in the corner.

It was covered in well-wishing cards, dried flowers, and hummingbird figurines. I found a shortbread cookie tin and opened it. Inside was a long dark ponytail, thick and speckled with strands of white. I ran my hand along it slowly. Her hair was course and dense. I turned to the mirror, held the ponytail against the back of my neck, ran it along my shoulder.

IN GRADE 7, we'd had a class trip to the Talbot museum. In a town with a population of 6,500 there wasn't much history to brag about, but the museum prided itself on its extensive collection of Victorian hair wreaths. The other kids thought the wreaths were gross, but Lionel and I thought they were beautiful—the various shades of black, brown, and blond all looped and twisted and woven together as intricately as lace to form flowers and organic shapes and patterns.

"Women would trade hair with their friends and neighbours," the curator said reverently, "to add colour and texture to their pieces." I loved the thought of that—various pieces of friends and family woven together to make an heirloom. They were also used as a form of mourning art. Sometimes strands of the hair of a dead loved one were wrapped into tiny pieces of jewellery. Lionel said it was weird since hair is something that grows but is made up of dead cells. Apparently, he said, hair can still grow after someone dies.

I told Lionel I was going to make one. I went home and started to collect the hair from my brush, tenderly pulling the strands straight into long strips, curling them in large loops and storing them in an unused pencil case. I was religious about it for a week and was about to start asking other people for their unwanted hair when my mom found the collection, told me hair is dirty and said it's disgusting to keep it.

I PUT MRS. Crane's ponytail back in the cookie tin, and put the cookie tin in the pocket of my hoodie. It bounced gently against my belly button as I climbed up and down the stepping stool to reach the tops of the mirrors. Every creak from the ceiling made me look to the door, just in case Lionel came in. I kept dreading that door opening, and yet I was disappointed when it never did. I didn't tell my mom I was keeping the cookie tin for the time being. I took it home and put it on my dresser, beside my collection of postcards from Lionel.

The trick to writing along a whole roll of tape is to empty one roll, and then start rewrapping the other roll onto the empty cardboard centre. I lay on my bed that evening and threw my ball of extra masking tape against the ceiling and waited the few seconds for it to fall while I tried to think of things to write to Lionel—about the collection of creepy wax dolls I had to dust every week, about the man who wouldn't let me throw out the mouldy bread he was saving for the ducks, about all the things I loved about his mom, all the things he got from her like her grace. And how I was so eternally sorry. I put five permanent stamps on it, wrote his name and address, and dropped it in the mailbox on my way to school the next day.

MOOD RING

ALEESA PRINS HAD NO ARMPIT hair. She told me once—or did Tyler tell me? Not even a little peach fuzz. At the time I felt it made her seem more evolved, like she had total power over her body. Also more infantile. For the entire year we shared a room, every time I'd shave my own prickly pits in the shower before running to class with wet hair, I'd blame her for the stinging red dots when I swiped antiperspirant against them.

I never pretended I wasn't envious of Aleesa Prins. It wasn't painful because I didn't lie to myself about it. I would have told her to her face, had she cared to ask.

She and Tyler would fool around after band practice under her pink comforter with hand-stencilled peace signs all over it—nothing too serious, he said. We're all too young to get serious.

You would think she'd hardly be able to play the triangle, but some guy with Sun-In highlights and torn jeans had met her at a mixer in the first month of school and offered to teach her to play his bass guitar. Even half-wasted she got pretty good after one night of practice. He lent her the bass for the year, and she would play it unplugged in the afternoon. Its soft and tinny sound quivered through the air between us while she tucked herself away in her corner of the room.

Tyler met me at our dorm one Saturday morning to go yard sale-ing for vintage action figures, as we had done once a month at home in Talbot. But when he heard Aleesa playing bass he went back to his dorm and grabbed his guitar and by the time the afternoon rolled around she was the new and only girl in his band. There wasn't much she would say no to. It was her idea to call the band the Ne'er-Do-Wells. I went to every one of their gigs that year, as I had for all of Tyler's coffeehouses in high school, and he had for all of my plays, even when I was a lineless fairy in *A Midsummer Night's Dream*, with nothing but a plastic kazoo for a voice.

Their hooking up wasn't supposed to bug me because he and I had always been just friends, and because it was mostly happening in his room.

DURING CANCER AWARENESS Month in Grade 9, Tyler's mom had taken us to the Salvation Army to buy afghans, and then taught us to unravel them and crochet the yarn into hats for chemo patients. We spent the month turning blankets into balls of string, then resurrecting the wool into berets or toques. At the assembly at the end of the month, the student body gave us a standing ovation for our generous work. I felt we were changing the world.

Tyler lost interest in crocheting, but I kept it up, making the trip every few months with his mom to the hospital. When I moved away to university, I found the nearest hospital and walked down every few months with two grocery bags full of hats. I attached a little note with a ribbon to each one: THINKING OF YOU, it said in sparkly ink.

"It's beautiful," Aleesa said one evening while I was sitting at our table, procrastinating on a paper by making a red tam. She was feeling sick and had resisted all of the invitations to hang out she had that evening. "The way your hands move when you do that. It's like they're fluttering, or dancing."

I blushed. I hated that her words made me feel warm.

"I could teach you," I said.

"Oh no—I wouldn't be any good." I knew she would be, but she couldn't be bothered to be around me for the length of time it would take to learn. "I don't have the patience for finicky things."

"You've got patience. You're pretty good at getting your school work done."

"Yeah, well, I've got to keep my scholarships or I can't

afford to be here. I'm the first in my family to go to university, so. It means a lot to them I guess, or something. To do things differently."

"Than who?"

"Well, than *they* did. You know how it is—your parents want you to have things better than they did, but they don't know how to get you there."

I didn't know how it was, so I just nodded lightly.

"But I just wanted a good excuse to move out. You know—small towns, nowhere to grow. So backwards."

This time I did know; coming from small towns was about the only thing we had in common. But I liked Talbot. I liked being with people I had known my whole life. I didn't know what to do in this new space, how to find these things to do to connect you to other people.

"You picked bass up pretty quick. But then, it helps having a hot teacher."

She smirked. "Bass is easy, straightforward."

"Guys think girl bass players are hot."

"That's not why I learned it."

"I know."

"No, you don't."

I didn't look up from my crocheting, the twisting hook mesmerizing us both as it grabbed loops and linked them together, its delicate stem so light in my hands.

She said, "It really is beautiful. It's beautiful that you can use your talent to help people."

"It's not really helping them. Doesn't change the fact that they're sick."

She got up and walked over to her corner and started plucking at her bass. The rhythm was too irregular, and I kept dropping the yarn. I started to feel motion sickness from staring so long at the flashing red wool.

ALEESA WAS LATE for practice and sound check before the Ne'er-Do-Wells' first gig. It was an eight o'clock show on a Tuesday night at a bar with a grimy disco ball hanging above the green platform that acted as a stage. They were only allowed to do covers. I drove Tyler and Aleesa's bass. She had a paper to finish beforehand and was taking the bus.

"So she's still borrowing this thing from James, eh?" Tyler said as he tuned her bass. He sat on the peeling green platform.

"Sun-In Guy? Yeah," I said. He chuckled. Did he find Aleesa funny also?

"Does she usually take a while to finish her homework?"

"She usually stays up all night before it's due."

"I guess she's pretty smart."

"Well, book smart."

"What does that mean?"

I paused. "It's been a while since I've heard you play."

"She's picked it up pretty quickly, this bass thing. Is she practising on her own, or with James, or . . . ?"

"He's over a fair bit."

He nodded slowly, twisting a tuning peg. My reflection rippled in the shiny plastic of the bass. His hand moved across it, plucking above my lopsided cheek.

"It's too bad you can't do your own songs here," I said. "They always let you in Talbot."

"In Talbot people know you. But there's no point if no one knows them," he said. It didn't entirely make sense to me, but I didn't think he was trying to communicate anyway.

Aleesa's heels clicked into the room, long boots clinging to her solid calves. She said hi, dragging it out remorsefully with her head to the side. Her big eyes were pinched in apology.

Tyler jogged over and hugged her. The stage smelled like vomit and cheap soap from a dispenser. I tried to look out of the window and watch the people walking along the street while blond wisps of Aleesa's hair kept flicking in the reflection.

AFTERWARDS, THE FIVE of us gathered around the table where I had sat alone during their set. There were about ten other people in the bar. The guys stared at Aleesa intently while she told us a story about her high school ski trip.

"My Armenian friend's mom bought her some cookies for the trip and left them in a paper bag on the counter, only she grabbed the wrong bag, so when we got to the hotel, she left the bag on the counter and I opened it, and it was full of all these chicken feet—little claws sticking out everywhere. So at one in the morning we jumped the fence to the pool area and swam through the indoor-outdoor pool after it was closed and dumped the feet in the hot tub. In the morning, we went down, and the whole place smelled like chicken soup. There was foam all over the top of the water and the kids were all reaching in to grab the chicken claws and throwing them at each other. So awesome."

The guys laughed for too long. Too hard.

"Where'd you get the money to go on the trip?" I asked. The sides of Aleesa's plump lips went slack.

"My English teacher helped me out a bit. I had a big crush on him, actually. He was the one who encouraged me to come here—"

"Were you sleeping with him?" I asked.

Tyler's eyes narrowed. "Hey," he said softly. I waited for him to say my name, to touch me chidingly, but he didn't. "Hey," he said again.

"There's nothing wrong with it if you did," I said quickly. "I mean, your choice. It's cool. I was just wondering."

She looked at me with a soft smile, and sort of shook her head. It seemed like disgust, but it might have been pity. I didn't deserve an answer. My cheeks were burning. I wanted to take off my sweater, but left it on and pretended my neck wasn't turning red.

"So what other crazy things did you do in high school?" Tyler asked.

"Well, our biology teacher told us once that if you didn't sleep four nights in a row you would go crazy, and we wanted to see if he was right," she started. She must have slept with that teacher.

I WASN'T SURE if Aleesa started skipping band practices because she was forgetting about them or just couldn't give a damn. It wasn't bothering Tyler enough for him to say anything. Sun-In was over more often as well, standing behind her, arms wrapped around her and the shiny guitar.

A couple months later she missed a gig entirely. "You guys are so together, you couldn't even tell you were missing a bass," I said as I drove Tyler back to campus. He didn't say anything. When we got back he asked if he could come up to our room, "just to check if she's there." As we walked through the yellow stairwell, I tried to think of a time he had been confrontational, with me or with anyone. Nothing came to mind. I felt my hands get clammy imagining him telling her off, his face getting red, saying I was a more reliable member of the group than she was.

She was asleep and had left a note on the fridge under a plastic manatee magnet.

So sorry I couldn't make it to the Ne'er-Do-Wells'
gig. Turns out I'm pregnant. If you see him tell Tyler
I'll explain everything tomorrow. Love, Aleesa.

She had emphasized her name by underlining it with a curlicue.

But I knew she would explain nothing to Tyler or to me. Tyler stood beside me and read the note, then leaned his head against the buzzing fridge. I wasn't sure if I should hug him, if I should wait for him to hug me.

He pulled his head away finally and said, "Figures. Figured it had to be this important for her to miss."

"I can walk you to your dorm," I said.

"All good—I'm good," he said as the door closed behind him.

SHE LOST TEN pounds in her first trimester, which made the boys pay even more attention to her. Everyone was so impressed that she was still able to get to half of her classes despite the morning sickness. Girls came over and talked with her and then held her hair and stroked her back while she threw up in our bathroom. It constantly smelled like vomit. Tyler was sure the baby was his, and never asked her for confirmation. Sun-In Bass Player didn't seem to mind that Tyler was claiming it, and no one else seemed to care whose it was, including Aleesa. It seemed everyone else thought she was creating the thing all by herself.

For the next three months she kept saying she was keeping it. She wasn't getting drunk at parties, but she still captivated everyone as she talked about the benefits of breastfeeding, about how the fetus was the size of a grape or a plum or a grapefruit.

But the bigger she got the less she talked about whether to do sleep-training, and the fewer books on motherhood she took out from the library and piled on our table. By early spring she stopped talking about keeping up with school by dropping a course each semester, stopped making plans with the girls who wanted to live with her next year about how they would try to find a place with enough rooms for her to have a nursery, how they would watch the baby while she was at class, how they would find ducky wall decals for the bathroom.

DURING EXAM WEEK at the end of second semester she woke me up at three in the morning when her labour pains became too much to handle.

"I thought you weren't due for another month and a half," I said.

"So did I. Should I call 911?"

"No, don't bother—I'll drive you." I dragged my legs over the side of the bed. I pulled on a black sweater with the iron-on band logo Tyler had designed for the Ne'er-Do-Wells—a moose with antlers made of fingers—and left my pajama pants on. I noticed in the car that Aleesa was wearing the same sweater I was, though her moose seemed more alive over her plump breasts. She had straightened her hair and put on makeup. She must have been up for hours before bothering to wake me.

"I'm the first in at least three generations to not have a baby at sixteen," she told me between deep breaths. "At least I waited till nineteen." She tried to laugh at herself but it sounded like a cough. "I'm the first to give the baby up." She reached over and squeezed the steering wheel tightly, just below my hand. "So we're getting better," she said in a forced whisper. I nodded though I knew her eyes were clamped shut.

"I didn't sleep with my teacher, by the way," she said.

"I know."

"No, you don't. That's why I'm telling you."

"Are you counting the time between contractions? You should probably be doing that. Sorry I can't help you, but I'm driving."

WHEN WE PULLED into the parking lot of the hospital I asked her if she wanted me to call her mother. "No, thank you," she said. I drove up the crescent along the entrance, parked the car, and watched her wobble through the automatic glass doors as they gracefully parted for her. I idled there for a minute, thought about my exam that coming evening and then drove over to visitor parking. When I got out of the car I was surprised that even in the city I could hear the cicadas sing.

I asked at the information desk which room Aleesa Prins, who was having a baby, was in.

"Are you family?" the woman asked. I looked at her scalp, the dark grey shoots of roots popping up below orange-blond hair. I thought she would recognize me from the time months ago when I asked where the chemo ward was. "That's a lovely thing you're doing," she had said in a cooing voice to my bag of crocheted hats. "It's so important, young people like you thinking about other people like this. You're touching hearts." But now she didn't remember.

"She doesn't have any family here," I said.

"Did she ask you to join her?"

"I'm her roommate." The woman told me to take a seat and then made some calls in a hushed voice. I lay down across two vinyl seats, legs pulled tightly into my stomach, head propped on a few copies of *Chatelaine*. When I woke up a magazine cover was stuck to my face. I walked by the desk, asked for the room number again and took the stairs.

It felt odd to be at the hospital when everything was still. I stopped by the chemo ward on my way to Aleesa's room. The doors were closed and the lights were off. I noticed something red in the garbage pail as I left the hall. I was convinced without looking it was my hat. I didn't bother to stop to confirm, knew if I did, the tension in my stomach would climb up my throat and I'd be a mess by the time I reached Aleesa's room.

ALEESA DIDN'T LOOK at me when I walked in. Two round soft nurses were busy smiling around her, telling her what a great job she was doing, wasn't she strong, a powerful woman warrior.

"So you found me."

"It feels weird to be here so early," I said.

"Yeah, I'm sure you know this place pretty well. You're a saint."

I couldn't read her tone. Even now, with her mascara smudging under her eyes and her bulging body covered in a gauzy gown, vulnerable as could be, I had no idea whether she meant it or not.

"You don't have to be here."

"I know."

She let out a high groan, then lifted her hand towards me as if she had a question. I took it and she squeezed my knuckles against each other. When she was done squeezing I carefully reached between her fingers with my other hand and pulled off my mood ring.

"Can I see that?" she asked. She held her other hand

open above her breasts and I pressed it into her palm. It was black. When she was done squeezing through the next contraction, she lifted the mood ring. It had turned a bright greenish-blue, a colour I'd never seen before.

When the baby came out she didn't want to see him, but asked me to go look while the nurses cleaned him up. I stared from behind their chubby arms at his blotched and screaming face.

"Is he cute?" she asked. "Of course," I lied. The nurses beamed. She went to sleep.

I sat beside her bed and flipped through some magazines until a woman came by to do some paperwork. I gave Aleesa's shoulder a little shake and the woman told her she'd been a real trooper, just a real rock star, and it was wonderful that she could bring so much joy to someone else through all this. Aleesa sighed and said she wanted to make sure it was the type of thing where she wouldn't have to talk to the baby's parents, but if he wanted to find her when he was old enough, that was fine.

It was three in the afternoon when I got home, and I decided that sleeping was more important than cramming before my exam that evening. I woke up an hour later to a steady knocking at the door.

Tyler stood there, red-eyed. "Why didn't you—" He stopped for a minute and stared at the finger-antlers on my shirt. I tried not to breathe. "Why the hell didn't you call?"

"Call?"

"When it happened!" His voice had stopped breaking.

"I . . . I didn't think about it. She didn't want anyone."

"Right." He stared for a bit at the plastic ridge along the threshold before walking away.

He didn't ask about Aleesa anymore after that. She stayed at her parents' place for the next month and was given permission to write her exams in July. Tyler helped me pack up the day after exams and I drove us back to Talbot.

THROUGHOUT THE REST of university she and I shared no more than passing waves in the hall. She got her degree, and even though we didn't invite her to the wedding, she's been sending Tyler and me Christmas cards since she got married to some lawyer. I used to keep them on the fridge for a week, but now I just put them in a drawer right away, with the others from years past. She's a music teacher, the first teacher in her family. She and the lawyer had two blond daughters, and they're both in pink in the pictures she's sent me. In the most recent card, it was just her and the girls. "Chad and I split up," she wrote, "but it's amicable." "Figures," said Tyler when I told him. She sings jazz standards on Thursday nights at a local restaurant, and asked in her most recent card if we wanted to come out sometime, but I haven't gotten around to replying.

PRETTY PRAYER

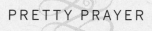

*D*EAR GOD, SHE PRAYED, *make me beautiful and deliver me from vanity,* which seemed like a good prayer because God could see she had her priorities right. She had just learned in biology class that skin cells die and reproduce themselves every month, so essentially she had a new skin every thirty days. She prayed this prayer before bed each night, visualizing her skin cells rearranging themselves while she dreamed (though she seldom remembered her dreams), renewing her face overnight. The old self gone, the new there to greet her when she woke.

She prayed this prayer every morning when she looked in the mirror and her old self was still there, tolerable but imperfect. And to prove her pious devotion to staving off vanity, after she spent half of an hour doing her hair, she resisted the urge to apply makeup before biking to school, to put a little shimmer across her lids to make her thin eyes pop, to take attention away from her crooked nose. She would prove to God she was different than the other girls— and he would heal her acne, make her A cup overflow.

If I should die before I wake, I pray my corpse will look beautiful in the open casket. She sat there in bed for a while, twisting a strand of her smooth clean hair (her one irrefutable source of beauty) between her fingers, imagining the people passing through the warm amber lighting like apparitions in the funeral home. How beautiful she looks, they would say—her classmates who had ignored her all these years, her teachers who hardly acknowledged her presence in class, the boys who she was good enough for but who always paid more attention to the flirty, high-maintenance girls. Her friends who were nice enough, but never appreciated how charming she could be. The young minister who shook her hand every Sunday and complimented her on her piano solo, and then reached to grab the next hand in line. At her funeral, he would be unable to keep from glancing every minute or so at her still, smooth face on the satin pillow. He would preach about the fleetingness of youth, perhaps, how man's days are like the flowers in the field, and how, as angelic as she looks here before us now, Family of God, we cannot even begin to imagine the beauty that surrounds her, that *exudes* from her in paradise. He would draw out *exudes* in the way a pastor does, so that everyone would close their welling eyes and see it for themselves. She's probably up there accompanying the angel choir, her hair swaying to the music, in a new and perfect body.

It's a shame there's no marriage in heaven, she thought as she played the stale piano in church, because she knew that there she would have a new body. She wondered how it would be. *Some glad morning when this life is o'er,* the congregation strained as she played. They always sang a little slower than she played. *I'll fly away.* None of the incessant blackheads dotting her nose, her ears smaller and closer to her head, her legs a little longer. And what would a perfect version of her face look like, she wondered? She glanced up from the hymnal to the pretty girls in the balcony, all done up in their flaring skirts and bright blouses. *I'll fly away, oh glory, I'll fly away.* They were moving their tiny painted mouths to the words exaggeratedly, and giggling to each other. Would she keep the length of her nose, but straighten it, shrink the nostrils a little? Withdraw her chin or stretch her jawline? *When the shadows of this life have gone . . .* Would she expand her eyes a bit, or would they look bulgy then, showing too much of the whites so she would have a permanently scared expression? Wouldn't that be something, to appear constantly afraid in heaven. *When I die, hallelujah by and by*—What if God defined perfect differently than she did, made her what he considered immaculate, but far from what she wanted? Would she then have to spend eternity in a less than satisfactory figure? Or if she were in heaven, would she be powerful enough to make herself look exactly as she wished?

"I've always been so glad to have a pretty friend like you," Georgette told her in junior high while they sat squished into swings too small for their sprouting bums. "I thought if a pretty girl would hang out with me, I must be a little pretty too." Their feet dragged sluggishly back and forth along the dirt grooves surrounded by gravel.

"You *are* pretty," she told Georgette, because it was a nice thing to say, and Georgette probably didn't hear that from anyone but her parents and everyone knows that parents have to say these things. It was alright to lie because she barely believed Georgette's words either. Neither girl had had a boyfriend yet, and she left Georgette for a fancier group of friends when they began high school. "I just have more in common with them," she said when Georgette had curled up beside her in the pew one day after church and asked why they never hung out anymore, her voice shaking, her eyes strained and red-rimmed.

BUT WHEN THAT *which is perfect is come, then that which is in part shall be done away*. That had been the text of the young minister's sermon on Sunday, and she woke up the next morning with the phrase running through her head. She said it over and over again as she rode her bike down the street on her way to school, twisting around cars parked and driving. The wind was catching her hair now, and she imagined that she looked beautiful simply because her hair was flowing in the wind like the branches of a weeping willow. The strands were dancing, were bringing life to her whole body, and she felt in that moment that it didn't matter whether God healed her of her ugliness, her brokenness, the pieces of her which were only part. In that moment, feeling a sense of oneness with the yellow and red leaves skipping along the street and the thin streams of sun between the grey woolen clouds, with the wind surrounding her, lifting her beyond the things of this world, she was perfect.

Turn your eyes upon Jesus, she hummed to herself.
Look full in his beautiful face
And the things of earth will grow strangely dim
In the light of his glory and grace.

It was at that moment, while she gazed up at the brilliance falling between clouds, that the man in the truck opened his door as she flew towards him.

"I'M SO SORRY—so, so sorry," she heard, and she could still see the streams of light, burning in a soft hollow circle of white, like a halo around his bearded face. Jesus, you see me, she thought, but couldn't will the muscles in her waking face to smile at him quite yet. It's alright Jesus, she prayed. I forgive you for making me this way. Now you are here, making me perfect. She forced the smile now, but as she did, she felt her lips press directly against her aching gums, and an emptiness along the front of her mouth. Still, as she lay there, and the sharp pain ran along the back of her head, there was peace, flowing thick down her cheeks, over her ears. She could see him in her peripheral vision, bending quickly and straightening, bending and straightening. She wanted to help him and as she pressed her fingers into the asphalt to push herself up, her hands burned and she felt a throbbing in her nose. "No, no! Lay back down," he said, turning to her, holding a blue cloth cupped in his hand. "It's better for your nose—I've called the ambulance—I'm so sorry," he said again, and his eyes grew wet, and he bent down again, picked another tooth from the ground, placed it gently into the blue cloth. She lay down slowly, ran the back of her hand along her dripping chin, and hummed her song as he collected her little teeth one by one, like the crisp snail shells she found in the garden when she was young.

This is what it feels like, she thought as they strapped her to the gurney, to be humbled by God. *Humble thyself in the sight of the Lord*, she mouthed. She saw the man hand a paramedic the blue cloth and wipe the back of his forearm roughly along his eyes. Her arms shook at her sides as they raised her gracefully, but she was not crying. She was shivering and her toes wiggled inside her sweaty shoes. She felt the ambulance jolt into motion down the busy streets. *And he will lift you up.* Now that she had the humbled part out of the way, she could be lifted up. The pain wasn't so bad. They would replace all of the tenderly collected teeth into her longing mouth, straight this time. They could restore her nose, reconstruct the nostrils into beautiful curves. A paramedic reached out and took her hand, and she squeezed it with contentment. She started to laugh, a startling laugh chopped every few seconds with a shudder. She pictured herself rising, lifted up, like the Assumption of Mary, beautiful robes flowing around her, hair billowing in the wind, eyes lifted to heaven, immaculately gorgeous.

MATERNITY TEST

"I'M NOT EVEN SURE YOU'RE really my daughter," Maurine's mother said to her, pulling her boobs into her polka-dot bra. "Sometimes I swear they switched you at birth. Because they took you and that other jaundiced kid from the woman who shared my room at the same time and put you in the incubators. Every time I nursed my baby in that first hour, that other girl was watching like a pervert, watching my baby."

Maurine just sat there staring at her mother's extensive nail polish collection, lined up against the vanity mirror. She knew some of the colours' names by heart: Jungle

Cat Pink. Champagne Fountain. Cherry Blaster Sparkle.

"She was jealous," Maurine's mother went on, "'cause my baby was nursing like a champ, and hers couldn't get anything out of her shrivelled, chapped tits. But of course the bitch blamed the baby for it. I think she switched the babies in the incubator and that was that."

Maurine grabbed a bottle of Sunlight on the Ocean and shook it till she heard the tiny silver ball inside shake.

"Not that it matters!" Maurine's mother practically shouted. "You know I love you the same whether or not you're mine. It's just that sometimes, when you get your asshole attitude on, like today, I wonder. It just makes me wonder if you wonder about it too." Maurine opened the bottle and breathed in the fumes deeply. Her mother spoke almost under her breath: "Because you can't love me if you're not sure you're mine. All that wondering makes you bitchy with me."

Maurine spread her chubby toes and began to wipe a bright blue coat over the chipping layers already there—Sex on the Beach over Sunflower over Midnight Madness. In that moment Maurine figured that, although the thought had never occurred to her, deep down she must have always known that her mother was not really hers, that there was no way she, with her chunky thighs and round face, had come out of this slender woman.

"Don't listen to that shit, Maurine!" her father said when she asked about it the next time she saw him. They were out for breakfast at Slim's Silver Spoon and she let it slip, the stuff Mom said. "Don't listen to her, Maurine—she'll drive you crazy. You know she says crazy shit just to get a rise out of you. Do you want to come live with me?"

And she did—Dad didn't yell, and he came home in the evenings drunk less often than Mom. She knew he would always have groceries, but he wasn't affectionate. Mom would say crazy shit, but she also said all the time, "My beautiful, beautiful girl. My beautiful girl," running her hands through Maurine's hair, giving her a foot massage while they watched TV. Dad had said "I love you" three times in Maurine's life, and she could remember each one as if it had happened only a second ago.

"Who will take care of Mom if I leave?" Maurine said, and Dad shook his head. "Now you're trying to make me feel guilty again," he said. His hands all cracked with tar squeezed the mug. "I'm not," shrieked Maurine.

"YOU COULD DO a pat test," said her best friend Andrea. Andrea was an idiot.

"Pat tests are for dads, idiot," said Maurine. She was sitting cross-legged on the bed, chipping away at her toenails with her fingernails. "I know that," Andrea said, watching her own knees as they sat on Andrea's bed. "I know, but there's got to be a mom version."

So Maurine visited the doctor with a fake cold and then asked the doctor about it. "I just want to know," she said. "I'm afraid that's very expensive," said the doctor. "I'm sure your mom didn't mean what she said." He put his hand on her shoulder the way a teacher might. She looked down at her hands and wanted his hand to stay there, warm and heavy. Suddenly she knew for a second that he was right. But then in the next second she shrugged her shoulders to make him pull his hand away—she knew he was wrong, knew her mother would never say it unless she meant it. "It's a tough stage in mother-daughter relationships, you maturing," the doctor said. He said it like ma-*touring*. He looked at her breasts when he said it. "Mothers and daughters sometimes say things they don't mean."

Maurine's mother was on the couch painting her nails when Maurine came home. "Come here, beautiful girl," she heard her mom say over the music in her headphones. "Come here and sit by me." A bottle of nail polish remover was tipped over on the floor in front of her.

"Mom, you stink!" yelled Maurine. She wanted to take the nail polish bottle out of her mom's hand and throw it against the window. She would do it if she knew they wouldn't get evicted for it.

"I just want you to come sit by me," her mom whined. "Take those things out of your ears and sit by me and tell me about your day and let me play with your beautiful hair."

"Maybe I would if you didn't smell like poison!" yelled Maurine. But she sat on the floor in front of the couch all the same, careful to avoid the spilled polish remover in the carpet. Her mom ran the fingers of her unpolished hand through Maurine's hair, as gently as a person could. "How was your day, darling? Did you have fun at school? Will you paint my right hand? I always do such a sloppy job. Do you have more friends? I don't know why you don't, when you're such a beautiful, beautiful girl." Maurine put her headphones back in her ears so her mother would stop talking to her with her wino breath.

Her mother took her hand out of Maurine's hair and smacked her ear.

"Fuck, Mom! That hurt!"

"What hurts is my own daughter won't even talk to me anymore!" her mother cried, and turned her face into the couch cushion.

"I'm not even your daughter!" Maurine yelled.

Her mother pulled her blotchy face from the cushion. "Who said that to you? Did your dad feed you another one of his lies? Another lie so that you'll go live with him? When did he tell you that?"

"Mom, you said it," Maurine said softly, now unsure if she had ever heard those words. The toxins in the air stung her nose. "You did, you did. I heard you." She spoke quietly, convincing herself of something that maybe had never been.

Her mother sat up slowly. "Come here, darling," she said, pulling Maurine off the floor and into her arms. Maurine felt her strength float away. Her mom pulled her into her lap, pulled her towards her so that Maurine's shoulder sank between her breasts. Maurine's sneakered feet hung heavily off the end of the couch. She could feel the many layers of colours pressing her socks against the canvas toe of the shoe. "Beautiful girl—what a silly thing to think. Of course you are mine," her mom said, and Maurine felt herself fade away again. "Of course you are mine. Of course you are mine."

THE MISSIONARY GAME

THE DEAD COW WAS WHAT launched my childhood insomnia. I lay in bed each night and watched the moon drift behind black trees, dreading the moment when I would see the strip of light under my door disappear, meaning my parents had gone to bed, meaning it was long past the time at which kids should be asleep, meaning I was not like other kids and therefore would be plagued with doubt my whole life and therefore would go to hell.

We went to the creek between two soy fields every day after school, jumping from boulders to the dried slanted banks of long grass, flattened neatly as if combed over by a giant hand. We played hide-and-seek in the outer edges of the woods, wedging our bodies under fallen trees and putting our faces against the smell of dirt and moss, climbed the crab apple trees and scraped off lichen with our fingernails, waiting to be found. One day while I was seeker, I stepped on the cow.

It had been a Jersey cow, with soft tawny hide darkened around gorgeous bulging eyes, except the eyes were eaten away and its sockets stared at me as if possessed. I stepped on a hoof and as I looked down, I heard the dark hum of flies. I saw that the entire animal was falling apart in tufts. There was a sickening swelling in my throat and I willed it to freeze there.

"Do you know what hell is like?" Reverend Thomas had yelled. "We don't like to think of hell these days. We want to think only of what makes us comfortable, what feels *good*." He drew out the word *good*, low and rattling in his throat, as if it were stuck there and he needed to excise it slowly. "But as long as we fixate on being comfortable—" his voice was rising, his eyes widening—"we're *destined* for hell!" *Des-tined* was punched into the pulpit in two swipes.

I wanted to plug my ears to shut out his vision of hell, yet I needed to see the horrors he described. The reverend's words kept my body motionless, buried inside his throat. "You ever seen a rotten animal before?" he said, nodding his head and drawing ours along with his. He spoke softly. "Roadkill, or leftover chicken that's been in the fridge too long." A few nervous chuckles. "Maggots everywhere, the flesh pulling apart and oozing . . ."

On the bank of the creek, beside the cow, the rustling leaves began to drown out the flies.

"Friends, there is no death in heaven. But in hell—well, everything's death."

A few cold drops of rain fell on the Jersey, on my arms, my face, stingingly cold. The grey sky was pulling in around the cow.

"Anyone here afraid of the dark? Sure—a few brave souls aren't afraid to admit it. But can you imagine, friends, perpetual darkness, never knowing where you are, not knowing why you are feeling such *pain*, such *agony*— not even being able to see the chains which tie you down!" He sounded so sad about this, his Jersey eyes drooping and the dry skin between them knotted.

The wind wrapped around the cow and me, pulling the scent past us quickly. The trees scraped against each other, and I could feel the branches pulling along my gut from the inside. The darkening sky was spattered with flies, fluttering blue through drops of rain between my body and the rotting flesh.

"See, we don't want to talk about hell, or think about hell, but we've *got to*!" He rose on his toes to say, "Because, friends, for those of us who know God *without a doubt*, we are in his kingdom for eternity! And there will be all love and all light and all peace. But if there's a place full of everything good and wonderful, ladies and gentlemen, there is a place entirely empty of those things as well . . ."

The first bolt of lightning drew my eyes away from the

carcass. I turned around to see all the other kids running towards the house. I looked at the cow once more then ran.

IT WASN'T THAT I didn't believe, or that doubts constantly buzzed around my life. It was that life was an eternity long, and how could I be sure I would have no doubts between now and the end? What if I made it the whole way through and accounted regularly for my sins and didn't embrace the comforts of the world, only to doubt God's existence on my deathbed? "For those who know God without a doubt."

So my parents would tuck me in at night and we would say together, "I pray the Lord my soul to keep. If I should die before I wake . . ." and I would mean it all, but what if I went to sleep and in a dream I doubted? After they turned out the lights I would lie there picturing hell, mad souls grabbing at my feet, pieces of my skin falling away in tufts, and yet always having more flesh to give, more organs for the maggots to infest.

"What if I go to hell?" I asked my mother after our prayers. "Why would you go to hell?" she asked. She seemed scared, or disappointed, so I just shrugged my shoulders and closed my eyes. "You won't go to hell." She kissed me on the cheek and turned out the light. I didn't know how to tell her I was afraid of doubt, didn't want her to know what my dark heart was capable of.

"IT'S YOUR TURN," said Jamie. We were playing the Missionary Game, which was designed like Monopoly, except that there were Providence cards instead of Chance, and Trials instead of Community Chest. "One of your supporting churches has withdrawn funds," the card I drew told me. "Give three hundred dollars to the Anonymous Donor Pile." I pulled three orange bills from my stash and placed them in the middle of the board.

"Do you ever get afraid of hell?" I asked Jamie. We went to different churches, and her pastor was a slight man. I couldn't imagine he had the strength to pound the pulpit the way Reverend Thomas did.

"No—why would I?"

"I don't know." I started to feel a little hot.

"Well, for other people, maybe," she said. She drew a card and read it out loud. "'Take your family on furlough'—ah, I hate furlough." She dragged her pawn to the corner where it was to sit until she rolled doubles to get herself an invisible plane ticket back to the mission field. "I mean, some of my friends from school and stuff—they aren't Christians, so yeah, that kinda sucks. But I know I'm saved, so . . . Are you gonna go?"

"Where? Oh." I jiggled the dice in my cupped hands, blew on them, and tossed them down.

"You're saved, right?" she asked me as I pushed my pawn four spaces through deepest, darkest Africa. I purchased a couple of huts and placed them in Zambia and Nigeria. "Sure. What do you mean?"

She tilted her chin down seriously to look at me. "You accepted Jesus into your heart, right?"

"Well, sure. He's there."

"How do you know? When did you ask him in?"

"I don't know. I just, I guess I try to do the right thing and pray, and stuff."

"Oh," she said, leaning back a little. She put her hand on the edge of the board slowly, indicating the game was on hold. "If you don't even know the day, you probably haven't done it."

"But, I believe it all—I pray before all my meals and before I go to sleep—"

"That doesn't really matter if you haven't let Jesus open the door of your heart." Her tone had suddenly changed. She was speaking with a voice I had never heard her use before. "You might pray and stuff, but how can Jesus hear you if he's not in there?" She spoke slowly and sadly, the way Reverend Thomas spoke when he wasn't being angry.

And it made sense. I was sweating now and hoped she couldn't see it forming along my forehead. I had always thought God was everywhere, reading everyone's thoughts, seeing if they were hateful or angry or lustful or greedy. But it struck me that if I hadn't invited him in, God wouldn't care what I was thinking or asking of him.

She sat there looking at me for a while from the top of her eye sockets, her lids hidden. I looked uncomfortably back and forth from her face to her hand on the board. Our two lone missionaries stood forlorn in the broad purple field of spiritual emptiness.

"Well," she finally said, "are you ready to make that decision?"

"To . . ." I wasn't sure what answer she was looking for.

"To give your heart to Christ? I mean, Felicia, I know you're a good girl. But that's not enough to get you into heaven."

I knew I should do it, but there was something holding me back. If this was the missing piece, what would happen if tonight I went to bed and still couldn't sleep?

"Once," I started, "when we were playing outside, I stepped on a dead cow—"

"That's not important right now, Felicia. Satan is bringing other thoughts into your head to distract you. You ready to do this?"

"Yes, I am."

"Okay—give me your hand." She reached across the open purple field, the five hundred bright bucks in the centre. I tried to subtly wipe my clammy palm across my leg as I brought it to meet hers hovering above the board. She fastened her eyes shut. "Dear Jesus, we know the wages of sin is death. But you died so that we could live forever." She squeezed my hand. "Now repeat after me. Jesus, I give you my life."

"Jesus, I give you my life."

"Forgive my sins."

"Forgive my sins."

"Amen."

"Amen."

I pulled my eyes open quickly, waiting for the weight of fear I'd felt across my chest to lift. She smiled at me. "Now I know we'll be in heaven together forever!"

She quickly leaned across the board to wrap her arms around me, scattering dice, pawns and multicoloured bills to all corners of the two-dimensional world.

"HEY, MOM," I said the next morning while waiting for my pancakes, swinging my legs quickly and kicking the leg of the table. "I got saved."

"Oh—from what?" she said, twisting at the waist to face me, spatula poised expectantly in the air.

"You know—hell." I felt like I had sworn. Suddenly the revelation of the term washed over me—we were all in one of two camps, me and everyone else in the world, from my family and classmates to the vague tribes in the Missionary Game.

She watched me as if waiting for me to say more, black plastic flipper in hand. "Yes. Yes you are." Her mouth became very small. "That's really . . . really quite wonderful! Isn't it?" Her eyebrows relaxed and her mouth drew into a tight smile.

"Yeah, I guess so."

She turned back to the stove and scraped the spatula along the bottom of the cast-iron pan. The sound made me feel a little sick.

THE STRESS OF hell lifted slowly as the day went on. But during the night the cow came back, still dead and decomposing, but walking against a purple sky and carrying Reverend Thomas. He looked down at me from his seat on the cow and shook his head with tender sadness.

"Still saved?" he asked, eyebrows raised hopefully, doubtfully.

"I . . . I think so."

"Think, or *know*?" he said deeply.

"Oh . . . know!" I sat up in bed. "Yes—I said the prayer that makes it for sure."

"When was that?"

"Oh—just the other day."

He rolled his eyes and the cow scraped her hoof along the dry dirt, making the same sound as the spatula on the pan.

"Just remember," he said in the throaty voice he used to draw out important words, "to stay that way." The Jersey looked at me from her hollow eye sockets, deeply concerned. Reverend Thomas wrapped his fingers around the cow's naked ribs, poking through holes in her hide. He kicked her sides with his heels and chunks of fur and flesh fell away. They turned and galloped into the incoming cloud of flies.

"Stay what way?" I hollered.

"Saved!" he shouted, and it echoed off the backs of the silent flies.

"DO YOU REMEMBER what time I was saved at?" I asked Jamie the next day as we paced the circumference of the schoolyard. I knew that dream-Reverend Thomas was going a little overboard, and couldn't imagine God would ask me on Judgment Day while the heavenly projector showed footage of all the awful things I'd ever done or thought. But I thought it might be nice to know, so I could give the man an answer the next time he showed up.

"We should have looked at the clock!" she said. "Well, you came over for lunch, and we were on our second game, so it must have been two-ish, I think?"

"Think or *know*?" I asked her under my breath. She had been the one leading the prayer so it was her responsibility to remember.

"So are you happier now?" she asked, squeezing my elbow. "Do you feel different?"

I didn't have the heart to answer truthfully. "I think I do, actually."

She grinned, and I felt a little resentful about being another star in her crown. "Nothing more wonderful than one more soul in heaven, right?" She had put on the strange voice again.

"But what if I don't feel it?" I asked.

MOTHER-OF-THE-BRIDE DRESS

EVELYN WAS NOT IMPRESSED THAT the yellow dress she was wearing matched the grocery store sign to a T. She stood outside in the sun for a few moments looking up at it, deciding whether to go in while people manoeuvred yellow carts around her.

No, she would not let this deter her shopping. Yellow was a good Sunday afternoon colour, she thought as she walked in and saw yellow stands, yellow walls, yellow everywhere. Yellow was plenty dignified and she wasn't about to let this low-end chain get the better of it.

Her skirt swooshed around her as she walked with a

basket propped on a large hip—a hip that had accomplished a great deal, that had brought two successful children into the world, that demonstrated she was more than content in her marriage. "Skinny women are the ones who are prepping the bait for their next fishing trip," she said to friends from time to time.

She used to be slim, back when it counted, slimmer even than her daughter Marianne, who upon getting engaged had asked her mother for her wedding dress, and Evelyn had brought it down from the attic reverently, draped across her arms like the Madonna holding Christ in the *Pietà*. However, when Marianne came out from the bathroom grasping the layers of lace and chiffon around her, saying, "Can you help me get into this thing?" Evelyn had smiled to herself, knowing that for all her dieting Marianne would never wear her mother's wedding dress.

"Oh, what a shame!" Evelyn said, lackadaisically tugging at the zipper. "It just won't do up. I was just so slender, I suppose."

Marianne kept pestering her mother to go for a shopping trip for "some much needed mother-daughter bonding time" to find a mother-of-the-bride dress, even though Marianne had bought her bridal gown without her mother present, and hadn't consulted her at all in the process. Marianne seemed to fear her mother would wear something that wouldn't look good in the pictures.

"Expectations for the mother of the bride are different today, Mom," Marianne said, and then waited for Evelyn to ask, "How so, dear?" but Evelyn refused to play games.

Yesterday Marianne had done engagement photos. One could hardly make a decision anymore without it being grounds for a photo shoot! When Marianne swung by afterwards to have a pot of tea and refuse cake, she exclaimed that she had learned "some amazing tips on posing for pictures. You wouldn't believe what a difference they make! I can teach you."

"I don't need lessons on how to put myself on display," said Evelyn. "I've run out of things to flaunt, and I'm quite comfortable just being me in my photos."

"It's not about being someone else," Marianne said. "It's about knowing how to bring out your best self. There's nothing wrong with feeling good."

Evelyn made her way up and down the aisles picking up berries, salmon, a rich cake for a treat, till she had to limp a little to support the weight of the basket. She bent down for a jar of pickled beets when a pair of lovely high heels caught her eyes, the kind she would have worn when she was young, but couldn't be bothered with now that she had nothing to prove. She followed the lines of the heels up the denim-clad calves to two perfectly rounded buttocks.

She knelt there for a bit, jar in the air, staring at this sculpted bum, like a button-cap mushroom, until it floated away down the aisle. Evelyn's basket was full and so she followed the bum into a queue before the cash. It was one of the longer lines—the bum had obviously made a poor choice.

Evelyn once wore such a bum. She had felt men's eyes glued to it as she walked by. But now her bottom hung in a sort of bewildered way, unsure of itself and so with every step she took it jiggled uncertainly. Wallace still grabbed at it from time to time, but she knew it was only to make her feel better. The pity of the whole display made her so uncomfortable that she would swat his hand away, saying, "Wallace, please. Don't be so silly."

When she and Wallace were first together, he'd kiss her everywhere they went, without shame. If they had been standing here in this same grocery store twenty-five years ago, he in his plaid cotton pants and she in slacks with a zipper up the hip and high heels, he would have kissed her right here, on the neck even! "Wallace, please," she would have said. And then when no one was looking, she would have grabbed his firm plaid arse.

So entranced in this imagined memory was she that she did not realize she was leaning forward and stretching her free hand out to cup the gently faded jeans before her. She grazed the memory of her own shape with her hand, the figure firm and forgiving of who she had become.

The young woman turned around abruptly, with a frightened look, pulling her bum from Evelyn's soft touch. She pinned her eyes directly onto Evelyn's.

"Whoops!" said Evelyn, withdrawing her hand, and the girl turned back around and shuffled forward. "Whoops!" said Evelyn again for good measure, and reached for the magazine nearest where the bum had been. She had no interest in this tabloid—"Pope's Secret Child is Russian Prostitute!" the headline declared—but it was preferable to having to look at the girl again.

She stood there until the clerk mumbled could he help the next person in line please. She raised her eyes from the magazine to see the little blue bum prance out of the yellow store.

As she stepped out into the sharp sunlight, two yellow bags hanging from each arm against her imposing yellow hips, she stopped for a minute to let her eyes adjust lest she walk out into the parking lot and be struck by a car, leaving an undignified mess of yellow and berries and broken eggs everywhere.

Evelyn could picture herself there, howling at the sun while people gathered around to help her, the girl with the tight butt returned and feeling guilty now for that judg-mental look she had given this woman who wanted only for a moment to remember what it was like to be squeezed and appreciated. There was something gratifying about the image of her lying there publicly howling, throwing dignity against the pavement, crying for all those things in life that were wearing and tearing in ways she in her heels and skinny wedding dress could never have expected.

She opened her eyes where she stood along the grocery store curb, and saw two warm smiles coming towards her. She recognized one to be that of the Pentecostal minister, though she had never met him. He had played Scrooge in the town's production of *A Christmas Carol,* and so con-vincing a converted Ebenezer was he that she considered attending the church just to see him prance around with reborn delight. She imagined him on a Sunday morning, romping around the stage as the Pentecostals do, saying, "I'm as light as a feather, I'm as happy as an angel, I'm as merry as a school-boy! I'm as giddy as a drunken man!"

She remembered now that he was the minister Marianne had hired to officiate the wedding. No one in the family had much interest in church, but Marianne must have shopped around and chosen him simply because he was dynamic and gregarious. Everything, even the wedding ceremony, needed to be a good show.

The pastor stopped before Evelyn and gave her a quick up and down look with his eyes. "My, aren't you just a lovely sight to run into on an afternoon like this!" he said, hands on his hips. Right there beside his wife!

"What a beautiful spring dress. Here stands a woman who radiates light for those around her!" He stood there and looked right into her eyes. She tried to smile, though the sun was making her squint in a way that might be mistaken for annoyance.

"Oh, that's kind to say," she replied. She wanted to take her bags and leave this undignified display, but couldn't seem to pull her feet away.

"Yes, it's clear you are a woman who brings delight to those around her," he said. And he nodded like a hen to show her he most certainly meant it.

"Oh, well, it's a good spring colour," she said shyly. "One can't help but look good in it." She looked to his wife. The wife smiled and nodded, not the least bit uncomfortable with the scene.

"Well, keep it up, sister!" said the pastor. And then he and the wife slipped past her and she was moving towards her car, flowing along in glowing yellow.

Evelyn came home and loaded her groceries into the

fridge, humming as she did. She heard Wallace's plodding footsteps along the floor and bent over with flourish to deposit strawberries in the crisper drawer. She stayed like that awhile, basking in the cool air and bright fridge light. She took one of the fresh, cute little berries right from the carton and put it straight into her mouth—unwashed!— swaying her bum back and forth as she meditated on the rich sweetness spreading across her tongue.

Wallace whistled deeply. Evelyn thought to turn and glare at him, but instead smiled into the coolness of the fridge until he came up behind her and gave her a solid grope with two hands.

EVELYN SIGHED DEEPLY as Wallace ran his hand along her puckered hips. She looked up at the sunbeams streaming across the ceiling and then over at the yellow dress sprawled across the chair in the corner. It had been at least half a year since she and Wallace had made love, and she couldn't remember the last time they had done it in the afternoon— certainly not since before the children had been born.

Now she got up and, remaining naked, put the dress on a hanger and began to sort through dresses in the closet. "I think I'll go to church this evening, Wallace." She pulled out a dress. "What do you think of this one?"

"Oh, it's quite nice," said Wallace, running his hand through his grey chest hair in self-congratulation.

"Or this one?"

"You look great in anything, dear. And even better without anything." He chuckled to himself.

"Well, I'm certainly not going to church naked!" Although the pastor might like that. Evelyn pulled the closet door closed with enough heft to make her bum respond with a jiggle.

THAT EVENING EVELYN walked into the Pentecostal church, Wallace in tow and still grinning. A cheerful young man greeted them at the door and handed them a pamphlet that read, SERMON SERIES: BE YOUR BEST SELF, THE SELF YOU WERE CREATED TO BE.

A young woman with blond highlights like Marianne's and sparkling eyes took the stage, welcomed everyone to the service on this very fine evening. She looked directly at Evelyn and smiled appreciatively. Something about her smile reminded Evelyn of Marianne in a way that made her twinge inside. She saw Marianne smile so seldom.

The woman began to sing a solo in a lovely honey voice. Her eyes were closed and her arm went above her head, then to her heart, then cupped the air in front of her. People around Evelyn hummed along, said "Amen" at the end of each line in the song.

The song ended and the people clapped, and Wallace whistled, and that was all fine with Evelyn.

And then, as if pulled to their feet together, the people stood up and began clapping in rhythm as the woman at the front began to clap above her head. The man at the keyboard broke into a lively tune and the young boy at the drums began to clang away, and although Evelyn did not usually care for heavy beats in music, she was drawn into this one. The woman on the stage kicked her legs from side to side in rhythm with the music. Evelyn pictured her in a wedding dress, the layers of fabric flowing and twirling around her flying ankles.

"Isn't this silly, Wallace?" Evelyn whispered in his ear. "Isn't this fun?"

The pastor and his wife stood at the front of the church, waving their hands in the air, their shoulders pumping to the music. Evelyn was disappointed that he was not jumping about and clicking his heels as Ebenezer Scrooge had, but he seemed to be happy enough.

The music billowed around them and poured out of the people. Evelyn was so swept away with the clapping and the swaying that she took Wallace's hand and began to dance, right there in the pew! Wallace's eyes were strained as if he were frightened, or curious, and so she turned away and closed her eyes and swung her hips. She shook and shook till everything was jiggling in a freeing way. The woman beside her smiled and said, "That's it, sister!"

The song repeated three or four times, and then Evelyn lost track.

> Towards the sun we rise, above this earth we
>   know.
> Light as birds we fly, leaving all our sorrows.
> With youth renewed we glide,
> with faith that moves the mountains.
> From glory to glory we soar,
> where joy flows like the fountain.

When the song was over, the people clapped and yelled all around Evelyn and she found within her head a voice she had not heard since she was a school girl yelling, "Glory! Glory! Thank you! Glory!"

THE NEXT MORNING Evelyn called Marianne and told her she would like to go mother-of-the-bride dress shopping. Marianne squealed like a child opening birthday gifts. "You're going to look radiant!" she told her mother. Evelyn closed her eyes, picturing the smiling singing woman from church.

"Oh, and I ran into your minister yesterday," Evelyn added.

"Isn't he charming?" Marianne said. "Just delightful."

"Yes, I'm sure he'll be very entertaining."

The store smelled like plastic wrap and Scotch tape. Marianne told her mother to sit on the settee while she fluttered around with a sales clerk grabbing shiny layers of beige and mocha and taupe and hanging them in a cubicle with a curtain. To think a place like this couldn't even afford doors for their change rooms!

"What do you think, Mom?" Marianne asked holding up a straw-coloured skirt.

"Well, it's fine if you'd like me to look like a wheat field."

"The mother of the bride usually wears beige."

"I understand if you'd like me to be invisible."

Marianne growled and turned to put the dress back on the rack.

Evelyn drifted around the room thumbing through

dresses like pages in a worn book. "Drab, drab, drab," she murmured, loudly enough for the woman at the counter to hear. Suddenly she spotted a bright chiffon swirled with sequins. She pulled it from the rack and marched to the change stall, but not before Marianne noticed.

"What do you have there, Mom?" she called. The rings screeched along the curtain rod as Evelyn sealed herself off. As she swivelled and shrugged her clothes off, she hummed the song from church the night before. She overheard her daughter muttering to the clerk, "She can't wear yellow, can she?"

"It's a nice tone for a spring wedding. Yellow is a nice subdued colour."

"Ha!" Evelyn scoffed. "It's the least subdued of all the colours."

SHE LOOKED LIKE a ray of sunshine floating down the aisle—isn't that how the minister had described her? She had thought it might be a nice surprise for him to see her there. He stood at the front, hands folded serenely, grinning gratefully as she waltzed towards him on the arm of the groom. All the people were watching her now, and when Marianne came down the aisle, they would turn back to her mother to see where her beauty came from.

THROUGHOUT THE WEDDING reception Evelyn flitted around the room stopping at the tables of guests, catching up with Marianne's friends and their parents. She walked straight across the dance floor, pushing past pods of dancers. The disco ball hanging from the ceiling sprayed light that sent the sequins on her dress sparkling like a hundred little glow bugs. She waved her hips as she walked to let everyone get the full effect.

At one point Evelyn overheard Marianne ask Wallace, "Has Mom had a lot to drink?"

Evelyn turned and said, "I don't need alcohol to have a good time!"

She looked at Marianne for what seemed like the first time that day, really looked at her. Marianne was wrapped in a dress that was not her mother's wedding dress, in the dress she had bought without her mother there, even though that was tradition. And yet she looked lovely all on her own.

"What's the matter?" Marianne asked. "Did I spill something on my dress?"

The revelation rolled over Evelyn like a breeze across a field: the bride's beauty reflected her own. Marianne reflected Evelyn and Wallace and the beauty they made together. It was a beautiful thing they shared, wasn't it? It was beautiful then and it was still beautiful now, maybe more so since there was more of her beauty. Yes, she liked that thought, beauty begetting beauty, and she got up and wiggled around the dance floor all on her own. There was a whisper behind the music that led her around on the dance floor, a whisper that said, *You are beautiful. You are seen.* Marianne laughed and smiled brightly, maybe with delight or perhaps with derision—Evelyn didn't quite care. It would turn to delight if she danced long enough.

TWO-TONED HOUSE

IT'S RORY'S FAULT OUR HOUSE is two colours. Mom calls the bottom Burnt Sienna but I think it's more like Blood-in-Your-Panties Red. The top she calls Sage but I tell her it's more like That-Thing-in-the-Back-of-the-Fridge Green. Mom likes to think it's artistic expression even though we didn't paint it. It was her on-again, off-again boyfriend Rory who spent an afternoon shirtlessly painting what he could reach of the siding, and then decided it wasn't worth the effort to figure out a way to make the rest of it work, so he left.

Mom works at the Kraft Dinner factory. My first day of

kindergarten the teacher looked at my Kraft Dinner lunch bag and Kraft Dinner T-shirt and said, "You must really love Kraft Dinner," as if she were trying to make me like her. "No, I love my mom, but we're sick of Kraft Dinner."

I used to love Kraft Dinner. I thought that's why Mom got a job in the factory—because she loved me so much and I loved Kraft Dinner so much. So we had it as often as I wanted. Then one night while we were eating she told me about how the cheese is grey at first and then they dye it orange. It still tasted the same, but when I took my last bite, I put down my spoon and threw up in the bowl. It was still Garfield orange.

I couldn't eat it after that, knowing it was grey, like the fog in the morning when I get on the bus after she's left for work. I'm paranoid about fog. Everyone has a phobia that sneaks into your dreams and wants to swallow you whole—Mom's is quicksand, Rory's is wolves. My phobia of fog started when I was five and Rory told me the first scary thing I ever heard. He didn't mean to scare me. He gasped when he saw it in the newspaper, a picture of a boy wrapped in the arms of his sobbing mother, his face hidden in her hair, her hand holding the back of his neck. I asked why he gasped. Afterwards I wished I hadn't.

"Don't tell her," Mom said.

Rory said, "It's real life, Jane. She's gonna find out anyway. The kids talk about these things at school." But the kids didn't talk to me about these things, and no one else's parents seemed to think they needed to know.

It went like this. There were five kids waiting outside

their house, which was just on the edge of a hill, and it was so foggy they could barely see the flashing lights of the bus's stop sign arm across the road. A man late for work was driving too fast to see them in time when he rolled over the hill. The littlest brother was off that day because he was sick. The only good thing about the fog was that he couldn't see his siblings from the window where he was waving goodbye.

Afterwards Mom was mad at Rory for telling me because I was mad at Mom for not stopping him. To make up for it, Rory gave me a toy pig with a plastic tongue hidden under its hard, felt-covered snout, and when you squeezed its stomach the tongue fluttered like the mouth of a whoopee cushion and made a pig sound. "Or a fart—I guess that's the sound pigs make," he said. He laughed. I laughed. It was a joke you couldn't over-tell.

Rory got Mom pregnant once, when I was eleven. She found out after Rory left her for the second time, but I wondered if somehow he knew. Maybe he could just tell and got freaked out, because there was something different about her.

"I don't know," she said at one point. "I'm a bad enough mother with just one kid—how much harder will it be when there's someone else to take care of?"

"If you were any better as a mother I'd be a brat from being spoiled rotten. And I'll help, you know. I'll take care of him. I'll get a job when I'm in high school, so I can help pay for food."

I was getting excited about the idea, excited and scared about holding a bottle to his mouth, about him laughing and spitting up all over me and me acting like it's no big deal. Mom would apologize for his vomit and I would say, "Hey, I'm easygoing," and just clean him up, and she'd be amazed at how good I was at taking care of someone, how it was like I'd been a sister since the day I was born.

Three months in she told me while prepping dinner that it was okay to tell people. I couldn't think of anyone I knew who would care. "Are you going to tell Rory?" I asked.

She slammed the Ziploc bag of Shake 'n Bake chicken fingers on the table. "It's none of his business, okay?" she said. "If you see him, you don't tell him. It's none of his business." She returned to her shaking, pinching the bag on each top corner and waving it back and forth. "It'll be enough work without him around."

I thought about my little brother all the time. When I walked home from school, I thought about what routes I would take to walk him to kindergarten when I was in high school. I'd have to get up early because it would be out of my way. I thought about how cool it would be to have him all done up in one of those baby wraps, his warmth pressed against my chest, his face leaning on my shoulder, my hand on the back of his neck. I thought about him when we learned about light in science class, how all creatures need light to survive, that it's a kind of food for our systems. I was thinking about him when Mom screamed for me one evening after dinner, and I ran upstairs to find her shaking on the toilet.

"Something's wrong," she said between sobs. There was blood on the floor. I dialled 911, helped her off the toilet, full of deep red blots. I closed the lid. She lay on the floor with her hands on her stomach, and her shirt soaked up the blood.

"How old are you?" one of the ambulance guys asked as they strapped her in.

"Thirteen," I said. Mom needed their attention and I didn't want anyone to worry about me.

"Do you have someone you can call?" he said.

"Yeah—I'll call my grandmother right away."

"Great—good kid. Your mom's going to be fine," he said, and then he turned to the guy with him and said, "She's fine. Lift." They carried the gurney down the stairs.

I sat there on the edge of the tub while they pulled away, lights flashing but no siren. I didn't know if she'd want me to scoop him out and bury him, or just flush him down so she'd never have to think about it again.

I tried not to cry because she could come home any minute. They didn't bring her back till the next day. It was the first night we'd ever been apart. I slept fine, but woke up tired with that awful feeling of recovering from a nightmare. I found out it's better to remember your bad dreams in the morning and be able to tell yourself your mind made them up than to walk around all day haunted by something you can't know.

She took a couple days off work, and I stayed home from school to take care of her, swept her piles of Kleenex off the table and into the garbage, pulled the plastic wrap off the sticky cheese singles to make grilled cheese sandwiches. I arranged soda biscuits on a plate in a pretty fanned-out heart but it slid apart when I carried it over to her. I took out some movies from the library, some John Wayne and Tom Hanks. But after two days her supervisor called and told her she couldn't take a bereavement leave.

"I've been there too," the woman said. "You'll feel better if you keep busy." I'd never met the woman before, but I pictured her with puffy hair the colour of red nail polish, hair I wanted to yank out of her head.

Rory came back later that year, around the time I got my first period. Mom was at work and Rory was reading and drinking on the couch and I didn't want to see him so I sat on the toilet and read until Mom got home. When I heard the front door open, I yelled till she came running up the stairs. She threw open the bathroom door. "What happened? Did Rory do something?"

"No!" I pointed to my underwear. "Does this mean I can have babies now?"

"No way in hell can you have a baby." She was panting from running up the stairs.

"No, but can I? I don't want one." She started to cry, still huffing. She knelt in front of me and put her head on my shoulder.

"You're a woman now," she whispered. "But you do not want a baby till you're older."

It never bothered me that she said this because I knew I was the best thing that ever happened to her, even though she had me at seventeen and life has been a whole hell of a lot of work since.

We walked uptown that evening to the Crazy Crazy Eights Chinese Restaurant to celebrate me being a woman now. On the way back she pointed out the doctor's office where she found out she was pregnant with me. We stopped at the 7-Eleven and she bought me a yellow rose. It sat on my bedside table till the head drooped and the petals began to blacken. I tied an elastic around the bottom of the stem and hung it from a thumbtack to dry on the wall, beside the carnations she got me after my first day of kindergarten.

It wasn't until two weeks ago, when I started Grade 8, that I wanted a baby; that I deeply wanted something that's a part of me to come out of me and need me and adore me. Rory was back and things seemed better than they had been before, till we ran out of food and Mom spent an evening yelling at him. It was a Saturday and Mom was at work. Rory had made Kraft Dinner for the two of us for lunch. I'll eat Kraft Dinner when Rory makes it, because he adds a secret ingredient, and it makes all the difference. He kept it a secret till this time, when I sat at the counter while he cooked. I tried to stay quiet, to stay out of his way, until he took the cream cheese out of the fridge. He scooped four big tablespoons of the stuff into the noodles before he mixed in the orange powder, stirring the globs around like foam in a whirlpool until they softened and spread.

"So is that the secret ingredient?" I asked him.

"Sure," he said, as if he had forgotten I was there. I could smell his deodorant floating around in waves as he stirred slowly.

I took my time eating, hoping he'd slow down too. I tried to stick one noodle around each prong of my fork before sucking them off. I wanted him to notice, to laugh or tell me to stop playing, but he wouldn't look up from his food.

A few hours later I could hear the familiar sound of him stomping around upstairs looking for the stuff he had left all over the house, and maybe some stuff that wasn't his. I walked over to the ghetto blaster downstairs, put in the Tragically Hip CD he'd bought Mom years ago. I don't think he thought about whether she would like it, just thought we should have more music that he liked, or more music in general. Mom never played it, but I liked to listen to it when she was at work, when just he and I were home, or even when he wasn't around and I missed him.

The music was so loud I didn't hear him stomping down the stairs. "You are ahead by a century," the speakers kept yelling. Rory was staggering towards the door with two packed duffle bags on either side of him. He looked tired. I wanted to hug him.

"I still have it," I said. "I still have the pig."

"What the hell are you talking about?" He swung a bag against the door to shut it behind him. I ran out after him.

"When are you going to finish painting the damn house?" I yelled. I could still hear the music behind me. There were dark clouds in the sky that wanted to rain, but didn't. It looked like it might be raining on the other side of town, where smoke was wafting from the factory. Rory kept staggering along.

"All you've ever done around here is this one thing and you can't even do that right! Can't you fucking finish something for once?"

A neighbour yelled at me to keep it down. I stood in the middle of the road and watched Rory become smaller against the grey pavement. I ran back inside, slammed the door hard enough that I hoped Rory could hear. I slid down the wall and tried my hardest to cry, tried to get something out.

I stayed there till Mom came home. She saw me there on the floor and started crying, "Oh God! What did he do to you?" She knelt in front of me and put her head on my shoulder. "This is all my fault. I'm such a bad mother—such an awful mother. The only thing I've ever wanted to do well, and I've gone and fucked it up." And I knew I was supposed to wrap my arms around her and tell her all the things I always did, that she wasn't a bad mother, that it's not her fault, that she's the best I could ever ask for and I would die without her, but I couldn't. I didn't cry. I stood up and said, "You're right. It is your fault." She stopped crying and leaned against the dusty wall and I walked out of the two-toned house.

She's wrong—she's not a bad mother. I just couldn't say it again.

I walked all over town that evening, past the school, past the doctor's office where Mom found out I was growing inside her and it was the worst and best day of her life. I walked past the grocery store. Three kids about my age were sitting on the curb out front digging into a box of

Chapman's ice cream with plastic spoons. They were huddled together, holding it above their feet, trying to finish it before it melted. I walked past them, close enough to touch them, but they didn't notice. They were laughing, wincing with brain freeze, running their wrists across their chins to catch the drips.

We haven't changed. She comes back from work smelling like grey processed cheese and I ask her how her day was. But now she just says, "Oh, fine," and doesn't tell me about the drama of the co-worker who is back in rehab or the guy who drove the loader into the wall so they couldn't work for hours or Frances who keeps falling asleep standing up so Mom has to work her portion. She doesn't tell me about those things, and I don't rush home from school in case she's off early. I don't feel the need to tell her that Jennica is getting super close—and not in a good way—with the music teacher or that Mrs. Webb turns pink every time she has to say intercourse in sex ed.

Mom and I don't talk the same and things don't feel right. And I know I can make a baby. And I want one, so fucking bad.

PLOUGHSHARES INTO SWORDS

WHEN BILL'S WIFE DIED I knew that Jinny would marry him. Apparently at the wake when she stretched her long pale arms around his neck and leaned into his blotched red face he whispered in her ear, "Wait for me," but not so quietly that Rosa Seemly didn't hear. By the time she and I were in the church hallway wiping shortbread crumbs from our lips with one hand and holding teacups in the other, Rosa'd filled me in on it. "And the look on her face! She tried to look sad for him, but triumph—that girl feels *triumphant* now, is all I could think."

And so when he called her up a month or two after the accident "just to talk," she went over to his place and made him cocoa and sprinkled icing sugar on top of the brown foam, and he put the moves on her, just like that. Jinny told me she pushed his hand from her knee and he dumped his cocoa everywhere, and she said, "I'm not going to be your rebound girl. We're too close for that. We're going to do this the proper way." And she got up and left with the promise that she'd be there for him once he'd sufficiently mourned.

So she was there the next week making bacon and eggs for brunch, and she made sure to put little bits of parsley in the eggs, just like her mom did when we slept over at her house as kids and talked about whether it was possible to stay in love with someone forever until we couldn't keep our eyes open anymore.

After that they weren't officially together, but they were never really apart either.

We were all a little surprised that he hadn't married her in the first place, seeing as they'd been such close friends all through high school. They never got physical or anything. But when we ate lunch spread out along the hill behind the school, he always made sure to smear a dandelion across her face that left a little stain like a token on her cheek before she'd shriek and throw a handful of grass at him. She made him little figurines of elephants and lions out of pipe cleaners and twigs, and once I noticed he'd taped them all over the inside of his locker door.

But she was maybe a little too headstrong for him. Francine was buxom with perfect curls and had that shyness that guys like in girls, the kind where she's pretty and quiet and doesn't ever need to say anything to draw attention to herself. Not that Jinny's not nice to look at, but her chin juts out just a bit, and she's almost as tall as him and if she weren't smiling, you wouldn't notice her in a crowd.

Besides, Bill was from a normal farming family and Jinny had always been an artist. In high school she sewed flags into her jeans and embroidered doves onto her shirts and after Bill taught her how to whittle, his hands around her hands as she wielded the tiny knife along a block of wood, she turned her desk into a labyrinth of flowers and birds. It was so beautiful the teachers couldn't get mad, although they did start checking her knapsack for knives.

Now Jinny was a folk artist who made sculptures out of whatever anyone in the town considered junk—dented tin pots, worn-out tires, retired bicycles. People would drop stuff off at her place and leave it in her yard, offerings in hopes that she would create something else interesting for us to admire or roll our eyes at as we drove by.

So Jinny and Bill got married in May a year after Francine's death and they just wanted a small event. She knit herself a white dress. The reception was in the church basement, which Jinny draped with colourful mesh and decorated with butterflies she made with vines and duck feathers. We in the Ladies' Auxiliary made our cabbage rolls and angel hair pasta with meatballs. There was a skit set ten years in the future where the pastor dressed as Jinny and his wife as Bill and Bill-the-pastor's-wife did all the cooking and Jinny-the-pastor stayed in pajamas all day yelling orders from the bed and it was all a good time. There was a lot of laughing and hollering and to look at Bill you'd never know he'd had such heartache.

We all wondered how Jinny would fare with the move. Over the years she had erected large figures all over her lawn—birds made of watering cans, giraffes made of brooms. She had an elephant made out of Mr. Pointer's old claw-foot bathtub, garbage can lids as ears, a plastic tube for a trunk, all painted blue with bright eyes and a half-moon smile under its pickaxe tusks. She made a fence with log posts, each one painted with a chipper face, a little dress or suit, and some sort of hat no one in the town would be caught dead in. The kids liked to walk by after school and try to figure out which ones were their parents.

There were so many creations we wondered if, when she and Bill got married, she'd force him to move from his farm to her place so she wouldn't have to part with all of her art.

But sure enough she moved into his big farmhouse, with the neat flower gardens that Francine used to care for flanking the house and surrounding the yard. Marigolds lined the edges and then there were black-eyed Susans and tiger lilies and zinnias and you name it. Jinny's garden contained tea cups on iron stems and dragonflies made of driftwood.

Jinny waited till they were married to try selling her

home. After all, she said, "There's no way I'm moving in before the wedding." She knew it would be a challenge to sell the house as is—the yellow siding painted with blue and red flowers, the interior just as ornate. "But heck, if I like it, someone else is bound to."

"It'll never sell, Jinny," Bill told her. "You've done some lovely work on that place but it'll never sell."

It was during the second week back from their honeymoon to Stratford that Jinny came over to see me. She kicked off her boots at the door and I asked her if they had seen a play and if she liked the swans on the river. She said, "Yes to the first, and no to the second," and then just stared down the table till I feared she would do it damage. I made the tea, and I didn't think she was going to talk at all. It's always a tough thing knowing whether to rant about your husband when you haven't done it before, but once you practise a little, you figure it all out.

"I'm just . . . not used to it," said Jinny. "Not used to making life work with someone else. And her eyes—that woman's eyes all over the house in little pictures drives me batty. Thank God they didn't have any kids so I don't also have their big, sad, guilt-mongering eyes to look at all the time." She sighed deeply and I jingled the tiny silver spoon around in my ceramic mug.

Turns out Bill had never stopped loving Jinny. "He told me a month after she died," she said, pressing her finger against tiny bits of sugar around the sugar jar, then licking them off her fingertip. But what was she supposed to do with that, she wanted to know.

"I mean, at first it was all romantic. I was the one the whole way along and he just made a mistake. A big old mistake and now things can be the way they should have been all along."

And that's the way she kept thinking all through their courtship. What else could she think? She was in love, again, and all that anger she had felt on account of him marrying wrong could be forgiven.

"But forgiving is harder than all that," I ventured, running my finger along the embossed top of the tiny spoon. Funny things, little spoons. Good for nothing but putting bits of sugar in your tea, and looking cute.

"No, that's not it," she said. "The forgiving was hard, but I did it years ago. And besides, back then I wasn't ready to be married. I pushed him away—not with my words, but with my attitude. Like a cat that wants you to pet it but goes and hides under the cabinet. There's only so long you can kneel at the cabinet holding sardines before you give up and eat the sardines yourself." She had run out of sugar granules on the table, so she poured herself another cup of tea and lazily dumped two more heaping spoonfuls of sugar into her cup, making sure to spill some on the way.

"It's not the forgiveness. It's the question of, what was she to him then? Was she second best, and he was still thinking of me the whole time as the best? Every time she nagged or was dull or didn't laugh at a joke or wasn't good in bed, did he think, Well, if only I was with Jinny. And now that there's no more if-only, can I live up to that? Or will someone else become the if-only?

"And what if we had done it right the first time, and the cat had not hidden under the cabinet but jumped on his lap and ate the sardines out of his hand—would Francine then have been the if-only?"

I couldn't quite follow all this but I thought it best to nod my head and listen. Usually if you listen well people wrap themselves up in their own conclusions anyway.

But she didn't. She didn't answer herself, and she didn't look at me for an answer. It was like she wanted to sit there in "if only" and wonder it away.

"Well, if you've forgiven," I finally said, "I guess all is well. You get to start fresh as man and wife. Nothing before this or after this matters." She nodded while she drew lines through the spilled sugar, watching her finger skim a continuous figure eight.

"He wants me to keep up the gardens," she said finally.

"Well, marriage is all about sacrifice, isn't it?" I offered.

"Yup. And I'm not good at sacrifice." She sighed deeply. I felt her eyeing the teacup and thinking about what kind of creation she could make out of it. "But I'm determined to be. Never do anything half-ass and I'm not about to start."

A week later I was driving back from the market and saw Bill out there at Jinny's house. I wouldn't have been able to see him in front of all those sculptures if he hadn't been standing on a ladder, a fat paint roller in his hand. The blue and red flowers on the siding were vanishing under stripes of dull beige.

I pulled my car up beside the chipper fence.

"Just doing some painting, Bill?" I said.

"Just trying to make things presentable," he said without turning to me.

"No one wanted to buy it as is?" Now that I was close I could see the flowers peeking out from beneath the first coat. It would take a while to cover those up.

"Who would? Didn't even bother putting it on the market till we painted."

"What about all these friends out here on the front lawn?" I said.

"Oh, God knows," Bill said. "One step at a time."

I left feeling a little melancholy about all those flowers being done away with, so I swung by the farm to check up on Jinny.

She was outside in the gardens. In her wide hat and floral print coveralls, she looked like one of her fence-post characters.

"What are you up to?" I said as I got out of my car.

"Sacrificing," she said. "Is this one a weed?" She pointed to a green scraggly thing.

"That would be, yes," I said. "Guess a lot cropped up since Francine was here, eh?" I said. Jinny glared at me. "Well, no sense in pretending she wasn't here," I said.

"He likes the gardens so that's what I do."

"How's your house selling?"

"Oh, not well. But Bill's taking care of the selling. Kind of him to settle the details. I can't handle giving it up." She wiped the back of a dirty glove across her forehead.

"Well, Bill seems to think it'll sell better now that he's painting it," I said.

"Now that he's what now?"

"Just passed him out front of your house painting," I said, and Jinny's face fell.

How it is people marry having never talked about these sorts of things I don't understand. Except that I think in the whirlwind of love and second chances we can become so afraid of setting off the balance that we convince ourselves that becoming one means we'll always want the same things.

Jinny stood there for a minute frowning at me or the sun, strangling the limp weed in her fist. Then she turned on her heels and ran towards the barn. It was past time for me to go, and as I walked towards my car Jinny blew past me on her bicycle.

I backed the car out of the driveway, and thought I owed it to them both to stop by Bill again on the way home. I didn't even get out of the car, just pulled up alongside the magical little yard and rolled down my window.

"Bill," I called, and he turned to me. "I don't like to mess, but I think I might have just inadvertently let your wife know something I thought she already knew, something quite frankly she should have known. And so I thought I'd just tell you she's on her way over."

Paint dripped from the roller down his wrist. I saw his lips move, mumbling something.

"What's that?" I called and turned off the car.

"She said she didn't want anything to do with the selling of it—said I should just take care of things." He wasn't angry. "I thought once the place sold it wouldn't matter to her what colour it was."

I sighed. "It's still hers."

Jinny pulled into the driveway on her bike, skidding in the gravel.

"Hello, darling," Bill said hopefully, waving at her with the paint roller. Jinny ran up to him, grabbed the bucket of paint and doused him in it. He stood there sputtering while it dripped down his chest and pants.

Having made such a mess of the situation, the next day I thought I had better check up on them. When I pulled into the farmhouse driveway, I was greeted by an army of thirty or so tin and wooden and steel creatures, their barbed-wire and garden-hose arms bearing garden tools that they raised threateningly towards the house.

Bill came out before I could pull away.

"What a sight to wake up to," he said. He sauntered over to the nearest figure and patted it on the head. Its soldered steel eyebrows glowered at him.

"And they shall turn their pruning hooks into swords," I said.

Bill chuckled. Then he said, "She stayed at her place last night. Only a month in, and already—"

"You knew who she was when this started," I said. "You knew it fifteen years ago."

"I know." He shook his head. "I just . . . I thought it was because she'd never settled down." He took the rake out of the angry creature's hand. "I thought she made them because she was bored. Out of loneliness."

I walked through the brown and grey menagerie with him. I stopped at a particularly endearing creature, its button eyes and curved spoon mouth making it melodramatically quizzical.

"With Francine," he said, "things were easy. She was peaceful, simple."

"Then why did you love Jinny all along?"

"I guess sometimes simple was boring. And now exciting is difficult. We knew what we were doing the first time around," he said.

Jinny moved back into her house. She painted the red and blue flowers back along the siding—they were never truly gone to begin with. Bill helped her open a folk-art store, because Lord knows the woman couldn't operate a business on her own. Some nights she stays with Bill, other nights he stays with her. His yard is tidy and he has learned to garden, though there are a few teacup flowers and hula-hoop butterflies among the plants now, and one little tin and wooden creature who hands him his rake.

HOLY OIL

W E WERE PLAYING FORT, AND I was telling
Danny what to do because I was good at it. "The
square cushions go on the sides and the cushions with
the endy things go at the front and back." He should have
known all this by now, but he was usually too angry to
remember things.

"And then you need to use the chairs with the hole
at the top for the sides so that you can pull the blanket
through, and the red foldy ones go at the back." As I tried
to stretch the blanket across the back of both chairs, he
climbed underneath and into the middle. "Hey—you're

not allowed in until it's done!" I yelled to him. He kicked down the couch cushion walls.

I yelled at him for a while and tried to tie him up in the blankets. He wriggled out and I pinned him against the floor. "Clean it up."

And then he did the thing he does: took a deep breath and screamed for as long as he could, took another deep breath and screamed again. Once, when Grandma had sent him to his room for pulling the shiny dark ribbon out of my Sharon, Lois & Bram cassette tapes, he screamed for thirty minutes straight. I held him pinned for three half-minute screams, his face turning the colour of the rims of Mom's eyes, and then I sprang up and let him run from the room.

The outside door slammed and I thought it was Danny till I heard Mom holler, "I'll be needing those cushions back on the couch for my shows!" She was back from her shift and switching off with Grandma, who would sit in the kitchen and read while Mom was out. Occasionally Grandma would throw a can of Chef Boyardee ravioli on the stove and then glower at us while we dug our spoons into speckled grey mugs. I imagined the specks added flavour, though I knew they made the mugs ugly.

"What the heck are you doing inside on a sunny day anyway?" Mom called. I kicked over another chair and grabbed a couch cushion in each hand.

I stormed to mine and Danny's room and slammed the door for good measure. I sat on the edge of my bed and picked up the only thing I liked in my room, the snow globe with the dancers I had gotten from Dad two years ago, when we used to see him more. I shook it as hard as I could. All the little dancers moved around in different ways as the chunky sparkles fell around them, bouncing slowly off their yellow hair, which was tightly pulled back and wrapped in perfect spirals at the back of their pin-sized heads. My anger was starting to subside, but I didn't want to lose the feeling just yet, so I clenched the globe again with both hands and shook it as hard as I could for a solid minute. I hoped the ballerinas would dislodge from their perches, but they stuck fast, shaking around on their posts. I shook it again and again, each time watching a different dancer. One would bounce up and down on a tiny spring. Another moved back and forth on the tips of her toes, her long extended leg moving in a quick arc, touching the shiny ceramic floor and then rearing backwards. Another spun in a small circle, round and round, and I felt nauseous watching her.

It wasn't because I hated him that I thought he was demon-possessed—on the contrary, I loved him enough to be the only one willing to do what it took to cast them out.

There were so many signs—the way he'd get so angry he'd hold his breath till he passed out, the way he broke anything of mine he so much as looked at. I kept a tally of the number of times my brother was sent to the principal's office by pinning safety pins to the bottom of my curtain. The house was full of traces of his terror: broken cupboards, soundless jack-in-the-boxes, the scars on my wrist from the time he had pushed me into the window and it broke.

The only reason for someone to be so destructive was that he wasn't in control. He had some evil spirit inside of him, tearing apart everything in his path from the inside out.

It was one o'clock and the day was too full of end-of-summer heat and I was too hungry to play outside in the afternoon, so I sat and watched TV from the floor while Mom smoked on the couch, filling the room with a white, spirit-like haze that matched the glazy brightness of the image of the Reverend Pastor John Orville.

"Go turn it up," Mom said, rubbing one hand through her short hair, which was the colour of a golden retriever's.

"Are we having grilled cheese again for lunch?"

"Just turn it up."

"And I don't mind telling you," the Reverend Pastor John said, hovering formidably against the dusty rose walls of his church foyer, "that I have *seen* the miracles of this little bottle of oil in my own life. It's a small thing, but I think we all know the Holy Spirit moves through the smallest of us, doesn't he, Mary-Beth?" He turned to his wife, perched beside him with her big yellow hair that sat still as a cage around her head, no matter how fervently the Spirit moved her to nod along with what the good Reverend Pastor John said.

"Yes, indeed, John." The corners of her lips moved up and made her baggy eyelids pinch around her beady eyes.

"Why, we have a nephew, Phil. Deep into steroids, he was. He's a good kid: smart, and kind, and full of life! But boy, that stuff messes with you. And for our young viewers out there, I don't mind telling you, don't even start with smoking, 'cause addiction is a harsh, harsh demon, ready to steal your life away." Mom breathed in her cigarette quietly as Mary-Beth looked at me and wiped a long pink fingernail along the black-coated lashes of her bottom lid.

"So our nephew got involved with these steroids, and I'm telling you, they changed that boy. Don't ever stop believing that the battle we wage is merely against flesh and blood—this was a spiritual battle for his soul going on here." Mary-Beth's mouth pulled tightly into a knot and moved to the side of her face as if pushed by an invisible hand. Reverend Pastor John took her thin fingers in his, softly folded like a bird wing.

I thought of the battle Danny must feel in his soul, this tugging back and forth of the demons and angels all rummaging around in his chest.

"He would be his normal sweet self and suddenly it was just like a shadow'd pass over his face. He'd lash out. You could feel that he was not in control of himself. Someone else was ruling his heart."

Mary-Beth let out a low, dark sigh, and looked down at the Reverend Pastor John's hand clamped around hers.

"So, I took this little bottle of holy oil to his house," and he drew it from his blazer's front pocket, "and I just felt the spiritual tension walking into that home."

I knew exactly the kind of tension he was talking about. I knew the feeling that things might just explode at any minute.

"And Phil came into the living room, and I asked if I

could just pray for him, and he was a little resistant at first, but deep down, he wanted to be . . . free."

"That's right. Freedom," said Mary-Beth, looking up, pinching the ends of her hair between the thumb and forefinger of her unbound hand.

"So I just wiped this oil across his forehead and claimed him for the Lord, not for Satan, and he broke down. Just wept! Well, I don't mind telling you he was a different boy after that. Altogether different."

"Freedom!" said Mary-Beth, and she pulled her hand from the pastor's, holding it up in the air like a timid bird, her fingers fluttering reverently.

"Miracles come in all sizes, and this is small but powerful. We pray over each of these, that they will bless our supporters, and with any donation to our ministry, we will send you one, right away! Because we know how dearly we all need a touch of the Spirit."

"Amen," said Mary-Beth. "Freedom! *Free*-dom."

I watched the ministry's address flash in a rigid font in front of their hazy faces and ran the words over and over again through my head, then ran to my room and wrote them down in my notebook. "Still want that grilled cheese?" Mom hollered from the couch.

MY HOLY OIL came in the mail four long weeks later. School had started back again, so I saw Danny less often and our fighting went from four times a day to once on average. Every day until its arrival I thought of it: each time Danny told Mom he hated her or called me stupid, when his teacher called and wanted to talk to Mom, every scream I heard reverberating through the drywall. When my heart began to pound with anger, I thought of the holy oil, small and potent, on its way slowly but faithfully through the mail.

I had spent many walks to school thinking about the best way to anoint his head with oil. I concluded that the stuff probably needed to sit on his skin for a while to let the Holy Spirit sink in, and I couldn't trust him not to wipe it off while conscious, so probably the best bet was to apply it while he was sleeping.

I had included a five-dollar donation in my letter to the Reverend Pastor John Orville. I came home from school each day, checked the mailbox on the way in and turned on the TV to catch the tail end of his program to see if he included my prayer request on the show that day. I wondered if my donation was too small to be worthy of the oil of healing, and started thinking about searching through Mom's stuff to find some more cash to send. She'd forgive me for stealing once she saw the results.

Finally I checked the mailbox and found a small bubble-wrapped manila envelope. In the top left corner was a return address sticker with an image of the Pastor Reverend John's smiling face beside Mary-Beth's stiff grin haloed by her stiff yellow hair.

I sat on my bed and tore open the lip of the envelope with a butter knife. Inside I found the little clear bottle, plastic, not glass, no longer than my forefinger and maybe twice as wide. Wrapped around it was a brochure for the ministry centre. I dug my hand around in the envelope, hoping for a letter, but found none, so I carefully lifted the little sticker from the top left corner and stuck it to my wooden headboard.

Danny was napping in our room. I crawled over to his bed, sat up on my knees and looked at his face, so still, so peaceful. Maybe the holy oil would freeze him in this serene state and he would never be angry again. The little bottle felt weightless in my hand as I shook it gently for a minute and then took off the lid carefully and dabbed a little on my finger. I tipped my hand above his face as slowly as I could and as lightly as possible drew my finger across his forehead. It was the nicest way I had ever touched him. He grimaced for a minute, but then his face relaxed again and he smacked his lips as I pulled my hand away. I had felt something. There had to be some change taking place throughout his soul. I had so much love for him in that moment that it felt like my lungs were pressing against the insides of my rib cage.

He opened his eyes. My heart beat twice, hard, then I thought it stopped for a few seconds. He turned his head quickly towards me and his eyes went big.

"What are you doing?" he yelled. He ran the back of his hand across his forehead. "What did you do to me?"

He jumped up and tried to rub his head clean on the stomach of my shirt.

"Hey! You'll stain it!" I pushed him away at the shoulders. His arms flew out, knocking over my snow globe. It rolled across the dresser, tumbled off and cracked against my headboard.

I ran to grab it from the floor. It was split down the centre and the liquid oozed through my fingers, thick and slippery. Danny ran from the room as I watched the dancers waver and teeter in their draining home. I sat on the edge of my bed, and turned my head to stare at the tiny Reverend Pastor John and his wife on my headboard.

I WAS STILL holding the dancers when Mom came in.

"What happened." It was a statement not a question. "Grandma said you guys were screaming at each other. She didn't want to come near—thought she'd get torn apart by you monsters."

I didn't look up from the globe. "He's demon-possessed, you know."

"What are you talking about?"

"I anointed him with oil, and he . . . it was from the reverend."

"The demon?"

I groaned. "The oil. The reverend on TV."

"Well, that man says some good things, but he's got some problems, turns out. His wife took all the money from the ministry and ran away."

I turned to her. "But she's with him on TV still!"

"You've been watching that? They've just been playing re-runs."

I turned and looked at their smiling stamp on the headboard. I leaned over and put my palm across it, not wanting to look at Mom yet hoping she would somehow notice the wetness in my eyes.

The next day when I came home, I found the globe-less dancers on my dresser. The glass was gone and so were the sparkles, but the dancers were there, poised in the air. I gently touched one's yellow head, and watched it bounce back and forth daintily for a minute before settling, still and upright.

BARN CATS

HEATHER HAD REFERRED HIM. SHE knew his older sister, who was "the sweetest girl ever," and if my oldest sister suggested it, it was nearly gospel. So when John Truman called, I said yes and he came to pick me up the following evening. It was my first date.

Heather lent me a brown polyester skirt. I kept reapplying my deodorant every hour throughout the day.

When we heard tires squeal in front of our house, Heather patted my bum and told me to behave. I responded with a scowl, and made my way out to the rusty growling pickup.

He rolled down the window as I approached. "Hey, you look nice!" he called over the rumbling engine. He reached out his hand. His fingernails were dirty. I thought of my fifth-grade teacher, the one from Trinidad who would walk up and down the aisles every morning and check our fingernails to make sure they were clean. If they weren't, he rapped them with a ruler.

I lifted my hand and he shook it hard, bumping his forearm on the bottom of the window. He winced. "Well, are we gonna have our date here on the side of the road or should we go somewhere?" he said. When I walked in front of the car, he revved the engine. I jumped a little, and my sweaty hands were shaking by the time I tried to lift the door handle.

He was laughing when I climbed in. "I'm so sorry I scared you! I was just joking around—trying to break the ice. Oh, but your face! You should have seen it."

Dinner was at the Capitol, the only restaurant in town with a flashing neon sign. Our father told us never to visit because the food was disgusting and the mugs were all chipped.

John told me about hay season, about castrating pigs, and about how they butchered in their shed even though they weren't supposed to because of "all the crazy health and safety crap." He asked me what my dad used to do when he was still alive, what my favourite class was, and did I like working in tobacco in the summers. I didn't love it but the money was better than picking strawberries. He said, "I think I'd rather cut the balls off pigs than work with all the Mexican immigrants, but you do what you have to do." I gave him short answers, and he seemed to appreciate that.

The food was better than I thought it would be, if you could get over the slight taste of cigarette ash. He finished his meal long before I did, and kept watching my fork move from my plate to my mouth while he talked.

He told me about their barn cats, how they loved to lick up the pigs' blood in the shed. Sometimes Scooter and Mittens would climb up the wood siding of the house and cry at John's window at night. He demonstrated, his hands balled into little paws hanging off the edge of the invisible windowsill between us. His little meowing kitten face had me snorting chocolate milk up my nose. He couldn't resist the little critters, and he'd let them in his room overnight. Then he shooed them back out in the morning before his mom found out the grubby creatures had slept all over his pillow.

After dinner, he suggested a movie. I would have said no, had it not been for the way he talked about the cats. We wouldn't have to talk anymore in the theatre, and besides, Heather had suggested him. We drove to Stanford where the theatre played two movies. I forced a giggle here and there through the comedy, to match his wet snickering. I kept my eyes pasted on the speckled screen when I saw in my peripheral vision his pimpled face turn to look at mine.

On the ride home, he rambled till he informed me he had to "go, if you know what I mean," with a wink. He pulled over on the shoulder of the gravel road, slammed the door, trotted past the front of the truck, and then to my surprise, wrapped around the side of the vehicle, passing me and stopping near the rear bumper. I whipped my head forward and glanced into the rearview mirror and caught him urinating on the back tire.

The next time he called, Heather told him I was unavailable.

BACON BITS

CALLIE AND THE GROCERY CART swivelled as one. She shook her shoulders in a spastic dance to make Aunt Lou laugh. The woman ahead of them was too busy texting to start loading her groceries onto the belt. Callie gave her a soft nudge from behind with the cart.

"I'm sorry," Callie said sweetly as the woman glared at her.

"Sure you are," said Texty, dropping her phone in her pocket. Callie would have shot something back if she had been at home. But in Port Franklin things like this didn't seem to bother her. When they had been at the beach earlier that day, a man had plopped down on his towel right beside them and started picking at the bottom of his feet, pulling flakes of skin off and flicking them in her direction. Callie-at-Home would have asked him if he had a problem—did he not realize that they were in public and not in his filthy-ass bathroom? But Port-Franklin-Callie just turned away and thought about the hours Aunt Lou had spent peeling the flakes off Callie's sunburned shoulders and lathering them with aloe vera.

"You mind if Dee joins us for supper?" Lou asked Callie as they settled in the car.

Callie pushed off her dirty flip-flops and plunked her feet on the dashboard. "Call her up. We've got bacon bits to spare."

Lou's best friend Dee had been scary at first, when Callie had met her three summers ago. Scary because Dee made intense eye contact, as if she could see your thoughts behind your eyes. Scary because she was quiet while you talked to her and she didn't make sounds like "yep" and "uh-huh" the way everyone else does, to prove they are listening, instead of actually doing it.

Callie finally warmed to her when they visited the workshop attached to Dee's hand-crafted furniture store, Wood You Be Mine. As Dee opened the door and fresh dust poured out, Callie finally identified the strange smell Dee exuded, the smell of wood chips and varnish. Callie wandered around the sunlit shop and examined the machines and Dee didn't once say, "Be careful" or "That's dangerous."

Dee took the wooden skeleton of a chair and showed Callie how to weave dried cattail rushes to make a seat. Her stubby fingers twisted the strands and wrapped them around each other, pulling them up and down through the chair's empty centre until it was filled. She made it look simple, but Callie's seat ended up lumpy with sharp strands bulging and splaying at every angle. Instead of scolding or lying that it looked great, Dee said, "That looks like a medieval torture device," and Callie and Lou laughed.

This summer Dee taught Callie to prep the rushes. They found a nearby ditch and cut down long green stalks while the cattails' soft brown bodies dodged their reach. Callie picked one and made purring noises while running it along Dee's arm.

"I think I prefer this thing to the actual animal," Dee said, petting the plant. "But I guess they shed."

"Should be called corn dogs instead," said Callie.

They stretched the reeds carefully in Dee's pickup and Callie sat in back, guarding them against the gusts of wind that threatened to pull them away.

Lou suggested leaving them in the shed to dry, but Callie was afraid the birds would shit on them. So they took over Lou's living room and set up a drying screen where Callie could turn them every day as Dee had instructed her, letting the air toughen their thin bodies, watching them turn from fragile green to hearty beige. The active waiting made Callie feel grown up, entrusted with something delicate that could become valuable in time.

After a few weeks, they sprayed them with water to "mellow" them, softening the brittle leaves. The next day Dee's thick hands demonstrated how to weave a basket. Callie took her time, slowly and rhythmically coiling the rushes she had cared for over the past weeks. They didn't feel dead to her but soft and refreshed.

"Now that's something I'd sell," Dee said, and Callie knew she wouldn't say it if it were not true.

"Look at your hands!" said Lou, turning Callie's red palms in her own. Callie winced and hoped that through the pain her hands would grow calloused like Dee's.

"Damn, kiddo," Dee said. "Should have given you gloves."

Callie said she would forgive her if she took over dish duty that night.

CALLIE AND LOU pulled into the driveway, past the plastic palm trees they had erected at the beginning of summer. Dee had said, "Thank goodness—there's a shortage of phallic symbols in the neighbourhood," and then later, "You're doing your part to help the snowbirds turn our beach town into Florida."

They were doing personalized pizzas for Callie's last supper in Port Franklin. She planned to spell a word on her pizza with the corn—maybe *jizz* or *derp*—to make Dee and Lou laugh when she took it out of the oven. She was going to pile on the bacon bits. Sometimes she'd pull herself up on the counter and grab the container that held a constant supply of bacon bits for Lou's Caesar salad needs.

She'd tip her head back and dump a few shakes right into her mouth. Callie-at-Home once had the container slapped out of her hand for doing this. "It's like you're an animal!" Dad yelled, and then made her clean up the tiny pink crumbs strewn all over the floor, crunching under her feet.

Callie tried not to think about home as she loaded up her arms with bulging grocery bags full of pizza ingredients—herb and garlic sauce in a squeeze container, roasted red peppers, anchovies in a jar, and garlic dills "just for the hell of it." Was it better, she wondered, to chase away the thought of leaving so you could enjoy the last night for all it is without the sadness of departure hanging over it, like a craving for something you've just eaten? Or was it better to remember this was the end and keep it there in your mind, like a peppermint tucked in your cheek during class, because then you could savour the sweetness of the memory when you needed it later, when times sucked and all you wanted was to be back here? Instead of screaming into your pillow, you could come back to the beach. Instead of telling the teacher to fuck off, and telling your parents to fuck off when they were screaming at you for telling the teacher to fuck off, you could come back to personalized pizza and Lou and Dee and the smell of aloe vera.

As she tried to open the door, Callie's hands began to shake under the weight of the bags. One dropped from her hands and she heard glass shatter. "Come on, Callie!" she heard her dad's voice yell in her head. She screamed into the warm breeze.

"Hey," Lou said coming out of the front door. "Hey, hey." She pulled Callie into a hug. Callie looked over to the beach, bared her eyes against the waves and willed the tide to suck up her tears.

"Why can't I live here?"

Lou squeezed her shoulder. Lou wasn't like the other adults who told you to look on the bright side, to pretend you weren't sad because they couldn't deal with it.

"You know, you're a brave person. And you're different than you were when you came here."

Lou pulled the unharmed groceries out of the bag, and then took the bag of broken glass and wasted pickles and threw them in the trash. No more was said about it.

After pizzas the three of them spent the evening dying their hair pink with Kool-Aid. Dee hated pink but went along with it because her hair was dark and the colour wouldn't show. But Lou's grey-blond hair picked up the colour vibrantly.

"Beautiful," Lou said, wrapping Callie's hair in French braids before bed so it would be wavy in the morning. "Do you think it'll stay?" asked Callie, running her hands over the smooth bumps of hair. "Well if it doesn't, you can just re-dye it," Lou said. "Maybe you'll want to try green next time." They watched *Bringing Up Baby* together, Callie pressed into Lou's shoulder, Dee on the other side, until Callie couldn't keep her eyes open anymore.

"Okay, kiddo," said Dee as she hugged Callie good-night. "Okay, sleep tight," as if she would see her next week and the week after that.

Lou came over and gave Callie a hand up. Callie emphatically pulled her ass out of her chair, and then draped herself across Lou's shoulders. They hobbled together over to Callie's bed, where she collapsed and Lou wrapped the blankets tight around her. Callie looked for signs Lou was getting tired of the dramatic display, but she didn't give any. "You better not write anything obscene in our breakfast tomorrow," Lou said as she turned out Callie's light.

Callie sometimes wondered how this all began, her staying with Aunt Lou every summer. It wasn't as if Lou and Dad were close. Even though they only lived forty minutes away they saw her just twice a year at holidays. Did it start that Easter when Callie threw a shiny blue Easter egg at her brother and her father slapped her, in front of everyone? It wasn't the slapping that bothered her so much as all her aunts and uncles and cousins seeing it, and then pretending they didn't see. Callie imagined her dad later saying to his siblings, "She's such a shit disturber," and Lou responding in such a way as to not offend, "Seems like you've got a bit of a personality clash. What if you two take a break from each other and Callie stays with me for the summer?"

Or maybe Dad had called Lou at his wit's end, offering to pay Lou to take her for the summer. And Lou, able to see past all of Callie-at-Home's antics, would say, "Of course you're not going to pay me." Perhaps years ago at a Christmas get-together Lou had watched Callie play by herself in the corner, abandoned by her cousins after pulling Bitchy Prissy Crissy's hair. Like the lonely, ugly child in the orphanage waiting for a home, Callie had waited for someone like Lou to see the potential in her, to spot the one child who needed saving the most.

Callie lay in her bed memorizing the glow-in-the dark constellations she and Lou had put all over the ceiling. Lou should have left her there on the couch between them—Callie would have slept better there. She could hear the TV murmuring in the other room, and got up to get a drink. She opened the door quietly, softly in case Lou had fallen asleep on the couch as she often did. She peeked out a bit and saw Lou and Dee sitting on the couch, arms around each other, faces pressed together. Her pulse thudded in her neck. She was afraid they would see her, and somehow hoped they would. She watched them pull apart, still staring at each other, saw Lou put her hands around Dee's face. Callie turned back to bed silently without closing the door.

She was stupid for not having caught on earlier. She should have known from the frequent looks between Lou and Dee, the times Dee would apply sunscreen to Lou's back and end it with a tickle. She had thought it was affectionate that they had both stretched their arms across the couch behind her head during the movie, but now she realized they were just looking for an excuse to hold hands. They thought she was dumb. They thought she couldn't handle their secret.

Callie sat up and punched her pillow. It was good then that she was leaving. They pretended they liked having her around because they felt sorry for her. She had had enough of adults who pitied her, who couldn't trust her.

THE NEXT MORNING Callie walked into the kitchen to find Lou at the stove, flipping pancakes with bits of spinach in them, the only way Lou could get her to eat her greens. Callie knew Dee would be at work, and although she missed her, she was glad she was gone. Had she slept over, Callie wondered as she pulled the syrup from the fridge. No one in the family knew; Callie would have heard the gossip if they did.

Had Dee and Lou been careless about kissing because they somehow wanted her to know? Was she the special one in the family, the one to bring their love to light? She remembered Lou's hands around Dee's round face. She couldn't remember a time she had seen two adults show that much care. That was the moment that could get her through the year.

"You know I'm going to have to put more syrup on them to cover up the green, right?" Callie said as Lou dropped a pancake on her plate.

"If you close your eyes while you eat you won't even know."

Callie closed her eyes, and prodded and chopped chaotically at her plate. She pretended to miss her face as she chomped in the air after her fork.

Lou stopped laughing when the doorbell rang. Callie's eyes snapped open—she hadn't expected her dad so soon.

Lou opened the door, invited him in, offered him a pancake. He glanced at the pile in the middle of the table. "That looks like something a frog would throw up."

"Dad!" Callie said with mashed pancake in her mouth. "That's rude."

"You're not even going to stand up and give me a hug?" he said.

Callie stood up and went over. He gave her a big hug, lifting her off the ground as he did.

"It's good to see you, sweetie," he said loud enough for Lou to hear. His flannel shirt felt soft against her arms. Maybe the time apart had made him gentle, given him time to forgive her for being such a brat.

Lou and Callie brought her stuff to the car while her dad ate the remaining pancakes. Callie searched Lou's eyes for a signal that she knew Callie knew, but there was nothing.

"WHAT'S WITH THE hair?" Dad said as they pulled past the plastic palm trees.

Callie clenched her woven basket, perched safely on her lap. "Dad, chill. It's just Kool-Aid."

"Hey, I'm just asking, alright?" he said. "Can't I ask without you getting all uptight?"

She sighed and pulled at her seatbelt, which dug into her neck.

"Just make sure it's out before school starts. We don't need to give your teachers another reason to judge our family."

She ran her chin back and forth across her knees.

"It's good to have you back, hun." He took a hand off the wheel and patted her knee with hard fingers. "Your mom really missed you."

Callie tried to think of things to tell her dad while they drove on in silence, some memory to share that he couldn't poison with advice or judgment. She could tell him how they had walked to the ice cream store every day for a week, just to buy the sugar cones, nothing in them. But he might say, "I guess we'll have to buy you all new clothes, now that you've pigged out all summer." She could tell him about trying to make their own hot tub in the front yard by filling a kiddie pool with hot water from the tap, bucket after steaming bucket, unable to keep it hot or to get the bubble bath foaming, and yet they sat in it all afternoon to make their efforts worth it. "Well, it's good to know that since I don't get your help at home, you work hard here," he'd say.

As they sat there in silence, she wondered for the first time if her dad was doing the same thing, trying to sift through memories worth sharing, or thinking up questions to ask that would chase away the weight hanging between them.

"So this year things are gonna be better at school, right?" he said.

She tugged on a chunk of pink hair. "Yep."

"So how are we going to make that happen? What's the plan?"

"It's just going to be—there is no plan."

"And how's that worked out for you in the past."

"Seriously, Dad. It's going to be fine."

"Is it, Callie? 'Cause you say that now and then you get to school and you go shooting your mouth off again."

"Fuck off."

"What did you say to me?" her dad said. He pulled the car onto the gravelly shoulder, slammed it into park. Callie turned away from him, stared out the window at the cattails swaying in the ditch.

"I said, 'What did you say to me?'" Callie pressed her nose against the window. The cattails bumped against each other playfully. They were beginning to shed, molting white fluff.

"Look at me." He grabbed her chin roughly and twisted her head to face him. She could hear a crunch as his elbow pressed against the basket.

Callie opened her eyes. She looked for traces of Lou's face in her father's. She saw for the first time the same confident jawline, Lou's lips pulled tightly across his face, the crinkles around the eyes where Lou's smirk was supposed to go.

"I don't want you talking to me like that," he said, softly and darkly. He unclenched his hand from her face, turned back to the road. "Let's not have another year like last year," he said as he put the car in drive.

As they pulled off the shoulder, Callie felt the sun against her face, against her chest, against everything she had been before she came to Port Franklin, felt it warming everything she was becoming, and she wanted to say something, something that would somehow break into her dad's world and show him that things weren't as fixed as he thought.

"Lou and Dee are in love," Callie said.

"That's ridiculous," her father said.

"What is wrong with you?" Callie said.

"You're talking out of your ass." He breathed through his nose loudly. "Lou would never tell you that."

"I saw them kissing."

"Making shit up, making shit up again to make your life more interesting. Just can't ever let things be as they are."

"That's probably why she lives out there on her own. She can't stand to be with closed-minded people like you."

Cattail fluff floated along the road in front of them. Callie looked at the dented basket in her lap. She had felt, in the few seconds before she said it, that what she said was brave and strong, that she was helping Lou be who she was, and that she was showing her father that for once it was he, not Callie, who just didn't understand, that his tiny world had no room for any of them.

But in the few seconds after, as she looked up at her dad's eyes in the rearview mirror and saw not anger or surprise, just steel, Callie knew that what she had hoped had not happened. That the Kool-Aid would wash out of her hair, that Dad would never ask his sister about Dee. Callie pressed her hands against the basket, feeling the brittle stems crack as it collapsed in on itself.

LOOKING FOR DRAMA

THE BOTTOMS OF NELLY'S STOCKINGS hang from the end of her toes, making her look like a Dr. Seuss creature. She kicks the ends of her stocking feet in the air as she marches around the dinner table. Nelly's twin, Timothy, climbs under the dinner table and tries to grab the loose ends flinging from her toes like crumpled moth wings.

Mommy has been making a new dress and Nelly will have to wear it to school tomorrow but Marsha will make fun of her because it has suspenders and no one wears suspenders. So Nelly tells Mommy.

Mommy says, "So I put all this time into making this for you and you won't even wear this thing?"

Thing is a funny word. "Thh, thh, thh," Nelly says as she kicks the yellowed bottoms of her stockings. *Thing* rhymes with *making* and *sewing* and *touching* and *stepping*, only in *thing* nothing happens.

"I'll wear it," Nelly says. "Can you take off the suspenders?"

"If I take off the suspenders I might as well take the whole thing apart."

On Nelly's twelfth trip around the dinner table she stops by the kaleidoscope on the shelf. You can look through it like a telescope, but it doesn't show faraway things — it shows close things, broken and stuck together.

Nelly knows Mommy doesn't want her to touch it, so she stands on tippy-toes on the ends of her stockings and tries to peek through it while it sits still on the shelf.

"Don't touch that," Mommy says without looking up from the stove.

"Can I show Marsha when she comes over?"

"You'll break it. You two are too rough."

Mommy dumps a can of Campbell's mushroom soup into the pan with the ground beef. Campbell's mushroom soup is the only thing Nelly can make. Twist twist twist the can opener with all your might so the lid pops off. Don't cut yourself on the sharp lid or it will bite every time you wash your hands at school, up to the elbow, singing "Row, Row, Row Your Boat," scrubbing till you finish the song. Pour the milk into the can halfway and fill the rest of the way with water, then pour into the pot. Stir with a whisk so that all the snot globs of soup goop go away and it is creamy with bits of grey like soft pebbles in your mouth.

Once when Marsha visited they filled their mouths with pebbles from the driveway and spit them at each other. The pebbles tasted like mud and made Nelly's mouth dry.

"You spit too hard!" yelled Marsha, and she went to go and play with Timothy. Nelly kept putting stones in her mouth and spitting them harder and harder until Marsha got over herself and came back to play.

"I like the suspenders," says Nelly, while Mommy stirs the mushroom soup into the beef.

Timothy quickly grabs the ends of Nelly's stockings and ties them together. She pretends not to notice, then stands up and wobbles till she falls. She crawls under the table where she rips off her stockings and whips him with them. They do this all quietly—Mommy doesn't think it's roughhousing, as long as they don't use their voices.

Nelly likes food with little things in it: mushrooms in soup, marshmallows in cereal, bits of peanuts in peanut butter. Little secrets that are good, not bad, not like the tiny bones in the fish Daddy caught when they went to the lake.

To get there Nelly and Timothy and Mommy and Daddy climbed down a steep path between two cliffs. Daddy went fishing in the creek while Timothy and Nelly walked along the skinny beach with Mommy till they found a stream of mud rolling down the cliff and then they climbed back up again, along the rough steep ground till they found a mud pit.

Girls should wear shirts even though boys don't have to, but at the mud pit Nelly was allowed to strip down to her undies and climb into the mud pit. She and Timothy played in the mushroom-coloured mud so she was wearing a suit of mud and wasn't half-naked anymore. If you reached down to the bottom of the pit you got clay. She made a small seal and a dolphin and Timothy made a bowl. Mommy made a monkey that sat on a branch with its fat legs hanging over.

Nelly and her brother pushed themselves through the mud and slid down the cliff in a stream of grey. The mud was shallow around them, till a big plop of it started sliding down and pulling them along. It dragged them down the hill and they could have drowned in the mud, but Nelly held on to Timothy and told him to keep his head up.

"We could have drowned!" they screamed at their parents when they reached the bottom.

"We almost died!" she told Marsha when they got back.

"No, you didn't," Marsha said. "You can't drown in mud. You're just looking for drama."

Imagine drowning in mud, Nelly thought as she ran. Imagine breathing in mud. Mud in your eyes and nose and lungs. It would harden there like the monkey on the branch baking in the sun.

Timothy and Nelly ran away from the mud pit covered in mud. They ran to the lake licking at the shore, where they washed the clumps of mud out of their hair and nostrils.

When Nelly ran shivering back up the beach to grab her

towel, Mommy pulled it away. "Your ears are still filthy."

Nelly pushed her hands against her ears and felt the secret mud, mud that was there but she couldn't see.

"Go back and clean them out."

Timothy and Nelly ran back towards the water but the sand was burning their feet so they ran over to the dunes. The dunes were peaceful and soft and had skinny trees all over them. Nelly scraped the crusty mud out of her ears as she climbed up a small hill of sand. When she and Timothy got to the top, they saw down at the bottom on the other side a man wearing no clothes lying on top of a woman. They were in the sand with the trees around them. This was a thing they shouldn't see and they heard them making sounds people shouldn't make. Timothy and Nelly walked quietly back to tell Mommy, but when they saw her she said, "Your ears still look disgusting!"

"You make sure to tell me everything," Mommy said sometimes. "If anyone ever does something you don't like, you should tell me. It's always right to tell me." But Nelly didn't tell Mommy about the people in the dunes because she didn't know how to say it.

On the beach there were places in the wet sand with dark rainbows of colour. When Nelly turned her head the colours swirled dark green and purple. Nelly wanted to take some sand home in a jar left empty from lunch.

"Don't take that—it's dirty," said Mommy. Instead Nelly and Timothy could keep the monkey. When the sun was setting, Nelly carried the monkey carefully up the hill, holding the branch, his back pressed against her bare chest. But she was watching the pink sky and tripped on a branch on the hill and the monkey fell underneath her. She picked up an arm and his hat and asked Mommy if they could fix it. But Mommy said there was no point since its head was broken. Nelly cried and Timothy said, "Mommy will make us a new one next time." She threw the clay arm at Timothy and ran ahead up the cliff.

WHEN MARSHA COMES over to draw, Nelly draws a picture of a girl sitting on the edge of a cliff with a beach below and water curling up to the shore and a branch behind her and a sunset in the sky.

"She looks sad because she's going to kill herself," says Marsha.

"No, she's not," says Nelly.

"She looks like she's thinking of jumping," says Marsha.

"It's a picture of you," Nelly says.

Marsha draws a big, hard X through the girl.

Nelly puts down her picture and stomps away to go look at Marsha with the kaleidoscope. She sees many tiny little Marshas, all touching together. Some are Marsha's forehead, connected to another Marsha's forehead. "You have seven noses," Nelly counts.

"Give it here," says Marsha. "You have twenty chins."

Nelly takes it back. "You have a million eyes, like a spider," she says.

"Stop it—that's gross," says Marsha. She pushes her hand over the end of the kaleidoscope so that all Nelly sees is black, and the end bumps against Nelly's eye.

Nelly pulls it away and puts it on the shelf. "Don't touch it," she says. "You're too rough."

"You're no fun," says Marsha, and Nelly storms away to her own room. Marsha should learn to play better. She is always looking for drama.

Nelly sits on her bed and draws pictures of monkeys until she thinks Marsha has been punished enough. She walks into the living room where she left Marsha, walks around the front yard, walks back inside and looks under the table and down the hallway till she hears laughing coming from Timothy's room.

Nelly creeps up to the door, which is almost closed. She peeks through the crack. She can't see them exactly: Timothy's back is towards the door and Marsha is facing him. She knows from the way they are touching it is touching that is secret. They are touching between the legs. And they are laughing.

"Can you do this?" Timothy asks, and does something to himself with his hands.

"Of course not, dummy," says Marsha. They are touching and playing and Nelly can see it.

Nelly had not told Mommy about the dunes and she knew it was bad and she knew if Mommy knew Mommy would be sad. But now she can tell and Mommy should know because there should be no secrets.

She waits till Marsha leaves without saying goodbye to Nelly. It is dark and quiet except for the light from the sewing machine and the *buzz buzz buzz* it makes as the needle runs along Nelly's dress. Nelly comes over and runs her hands along the suspenders hanging from the sewing machine. "Marsha and Timothy were touching each other," says Nelly quietly.

Mommy lifts her foot off the pedal so the machine stops buzzing.

"What do you mean?"

"They were just touching." Nelly feels the heat from the sewing machine against her hands. She pulls them behind her back.

"How do you mean touching?"

"Just showing each other their privates."

Mommy flicks off the sewing machine light. "Where were you when this was happening?"

"In the hall."

"And you didn't tell them to stop?"

Nelly's face burns. She hadn't thought about that.

"You obviously know they were doing something they shouldn't be doing or you wouldn't have told me." Mommy runs three fingers up and down between her eyes. She pulls the dress out from the machine and snaps the threads between her fists.

"Are you going to tell Marsha's parents?" Nelly asks.

Mommy gets up and doesn't say anything.

"Shouldn't Marsha's mom know? *She* doesn't tell her mom everything," Nelly says as Mommy walks down the hall to the living room.

Mommy walks into Timothy's room and closes the door.

Nelly walks across the wood floor to the shelf where

the kaleidoscope is, making sure not to trip on the ends of her stockings. She can hear Timothy whine something. She listens to the sound the kaleidoscope makes as she drags it across the wooden shelf. She listens to that instead of Mommy talking to Timothy in a low voice.

Nelly holds it in her hand. She knows she can hold it without dropping it and yet she knows she will drop it. She can feel it getting heavy in her hands. She can hear it making a buzzing sound, a sound louder than Mommy's angry whispering. "I don't *ever* want you to . . ." Mommy says to Timothy, but the kaleidoscope is loud and smooth and the smoothness is slipping from her hand. It breaks apart on the floor.

"Nelly?" Mommy calls. "Nelly? What was that?"

The buzzing stops. Nelly's heart pounds where the buzzing was.

Nelly steps onto the pieces, covering them. She can feel them burning under her feet, like sand at the beach.

Mommy walks out of Timothy's room. Nelly listens for Timothy, waiting for him to whimper. She doesn't want him to cry, but it would be better for him to cry than to be silent.

"What happened?" Mommy says.

Nelly lifts one foot and looks at the bottom. Blood is spreading along her cream-coloured stockings, little red spots turning pink on the outsides.

CAT FOOD TREES

I STILL SHUDDER WHEN I THINK of the story my art instructor shared of a painting she had poured herself into for weeks on end, a painting of a faceless woman against a grey background. My instructor's five-year-old son, whom she had been teaching to paint, snuck into her studio and with a Crayola marker filled in the blank features, giving the woman a thick crooked smile. Hearing her recall the painful event, finally with laughter after weeks of recovery, I concluded it was one of the funniest, saddest stories I had heard in a long time, and that I could never have children.

"My work is my baby," I said whenever someone pestered us about when we planned on having kids. That was usually enough to shut them up.

"And she has morning sickness till it's finished," Dave would add. He'd wink and I'd elbow him in the ribs.

It sounds cheesy but I believed that I could relate to the joy of holding a new child. Watching my sister in a messy, hysterical state, grasping her newborn son at her swollen breast, I truly felt I could empathize, at least in part, with the satisfaction and pride of having sweated and ripped and pushed after months of growth and slow development. Then finally to end up holding something that is part of you, and always will be, and gives you pure joy just to look at it.

"So do you find it difficult to sell your children?" my sister once asked with a twitching smile after my answer. You jerk, I thought. You've been stewing that one up for weeks.

"Touché," Dave nodded, smiling. I took the opportunity to glare at him as soon as she looked down at her belly in satisfaction.

"They've got to grow up sometime," I said.

It was easy to make the connection between procreation and artistic creation when I had only encountered the latter. The metaphor still works, of course. But it's different. It's like the time Dave walked into the studio unannounced and scared my heavy red brush stroke across the finishing touches of an abstract painting. The piece took on a whole new feel that I had never intended, and therefore a new meaning.

I thought I understood child rearing, could in fairness compare painting to parenting, until I held my own child.

REBECCA HAD A paintbrush in her hand long before she could speak. I began to fantasize about my daughter becoming a sort of artistic child-genius. One of her first gifts from us, purchased and immediately hidden but thought of often, was a plastic easel and a child's art kit, filled with edible watercolours, soy crayons, and scented non-toxic markers. These things were normal accessories to a child's collection, but to me they had the potential of a magic wand. All through the precious months of nursing, I eagerly awaited the day when the tiny perfect hand that clutched my baby finger would hold the stem of a brush and create wonder we previously could only imagine.

So, when she went through a stage of restricting her artistic interest to pencil drawings and refused to sit still for longer than a few half-hearted scribbles to appease me, I was forced to make great efforts to hide my pained disappointment. Try as I might to encourage and to teach and to create an environment conducive to creative inspiration, she would squirm and fidget and disappear as soon as she could. I hung poster paper across her walls, attempted finger painting lessons, gave her the opportunity to make all sorts of creative messes that any other parent would punish. Yet, she preferred to keep her hands clean; her easel was reduced to the framework of a fort, and the plethora of children's art supplies that had been at her command was left relatively unused by anyone but me.

I dreamt of bright canvases filled with splats of colour and representations of the innocent heart of a genuine (not merely child-like, but our very own actual) child artist. Of course, I never articulated these dreams to Dave; they would never survive my embarrassment. Or perhaps I was simply holding my maternal aspiration in such a deep place that it remained purely abstract.

Still, Dave can read my emotions painted on the canvas or my face, and, putting his arm around me after my unsuccessful attempts to coax Rebecca into developing her potential skills, he would coo, "She'll come along. She's still young. Give it time. Just be patient."

Repetitive positive statements. Like the ones we had been taught to hand out liberally in parenting class. In many ways I regretted having taken those classes. As practical as these interpersonal skills were, I couldn't help but feel demeaned when they were applied to me. Even though Dave was just saying things he would have said before, with that soft disposition that had melted my doubts when our family was composed of just we two, they now seemed manipulative manoeuvres designed to make me let go of my expectations for my child.

His excitement about learning to release expectations for our child had set my stomach off right from the beginning. "Wow," he said, as we walked home through the warm, darkening evening, "I hadn't realized how many expectations I had already—only a few months into knowing we were expecting!" He smiled, comforted by the new revelation.

I looked back at him, and pushed the corners of my mouth up to make sure he knew I cared. But the feeling I get when he tells me of a decision he made without asking my opinion trickled into my gut.

I could not let my expectations go so easily. It wasn't even a matter of *hoping* my child would follow in my interests; it was just the way it would be. Dave and I had made great efforts to keep our home a warm, learning environment in which Rebecca could grow to be all that her beautiful soul, packed with creative potential, intended her to be.

One particular evening, while I sat reading, the words I had said so often as a child, and swore I would never give my child the opportunity to say, somehow escaped my three-year-old's mouth: "Mommy, I'm bored."

At times like this, I regretted our decision to get rid of the TV.

"Well, sweetie," I said with my eyes lodged in my book, "what do you like to do?" This kind of question stimulates self-discovery, we were informed in our parenting class.

"I don't know."

This kind of answer never came up in class. Maybe in a year I could design an overpriced ten-session course as well; mine would give realistic scenarios.

"Well," I said, searching to further stimulate introspective thinking, "would you like to make something?"

There. That wasn't pointed or directional. *Make* is such a broad verb, but an inspirational one. She could make a story or a friend. She could make her bed, make a fairy-tale land with her toys. She could make a song. Or a picture.

"No! Mom!" she snapped. Rebecca switched from "Mommy" to "Mom" when angry. "I don't like drawing!" She stomped off to her room.

The words, of course, cut deep. My child didn't enjoy the thing her father and I enjoy most in life. My worst nightmare had come true: my child did not like art.

I couldn't announce such thoughts to Dave, knowing he would find my reaction melodramatic and premature. But my thoughts kept returning to the subject, picturing the future of our family ruptured by our progeny's distaste for our greatest passion.

"I think children are sort of like Pollock," I told Dave, late at night. "There's no rhyme or reason, no representation. And as soon as you attempt to dissect them, they yield something entirely different than you would have imagined." I sighed and leaned against his shoulder, attempting to reread the pages I had read after my daughter stormed off.

"You mean, kids weren't meant to be dissected?" Dave said absentmindedly, in his voice of take-it-or-leave-it wisdom. Today I decided to take it. I dropped the book beside me and snuggled into his neck.

The next morning I pulled on my kimono, turned on the coffee maker, and headed into the studio. I rubbed my heavy eyes as I stepped into the room to see a little brunette head staring at the easel. She still wore her pajamas. She looked up at me quickly, slightly embarrassed.

"Hi," I said, trying not to show my surprise. We had

always tried to leave the door open, to make the studio a comfortable place where our daughter would feel welcome to be an active participant or just a silent observer. I had encouraged her on several occasions to come in while Dave or I were painting or drawing, but she had remained disinterested, only coming in to appease us, and recently she had not even bothered to do that.

She turned away from me sheepishly, glanced around, and then looked back at the easel.

I tried to break the silence.

"You're up early."

"I was sick of being in bed," she said grumpily. She stared at the easel still.

"Mommy, what's this?" She pointed a careful finger at a corner of my painting, knowing better than to touch the canvas.

"What's what, honey?" I stepped up to the easel and sat down on the stool beside her.

"Right down here."

"That's a tree."

"It doesn't look like a tree."

The preschooler's mind is at the height of imaginative creativity, I recalled someone saying once. People try too hard to be deep, I concluded emotionlessly. I yawned and tried to shake my head clear to prepare for my lesson.

"That's because it's a Cubist tree," I said, still too foggy to try to think through ways of communicating that she would understand.

She grimaced and shook her head.

"It looks like cat food."

It was my turn to grimace. The height of imaginative creativity. "Well, thank you."

Her eyes scoured the canvas. I could tell that quickly, in her inarticulate thought processes she was analyzing, dissecting, critiquing my nearly completed piece.

"Mommy," she said with an innocently tilted head, "why do you work alone?"

I said softly, "Well, I would love for you to come in here with me while I work."

"No," she shook her head, slightly frustrated with my misunderstanding. "Why do you paint this picture alone? Why don't you let people help you?"

I sat silently for a minute. "Do you think I need help?" I tried to sound as unoffended as possible.

"You always help me. And your trees don't look like trees."

I had been looking forward to putting the finishing touches on this massive piece. "You'll be shocked by what your child will teach you," said the woman who had taught the class. Dave had smiled with excitement, which I deemed foolish.

"Would you like to help me finish this?" I blurted before I could fear the consequences. My empty stomach wasn't sitting well. But I felt a strange sense of relief.

She sat on my lap with the largest of my horsehair brushes gripped in a tight round fist dabbing irregular blotches of green and brown and gold over my linear arrangement of blue-grey shapes and shades. I bit my lip as, within a minute, she'd covered the tree I had spent hours perfecting.

In the end, it wasn't as bad as I had prepared myself for. Sharp delicate figures I had designed jutted out from between stripes and splats of abstract mixes of colour. I couldn't show it, but it was a start.

HAPPY ALL THE TIME

MARCUS HANNIGAN WAS A CHUBBY kid, but he
was also strong and everyone said he had great hair
so his weight didn't bother him, until Grade 7 when his
mom married Frank, a nurse who ran marathons. Frank
started switching the food packed in Marcus's insulated
Superman lunch sack from things like Fruit Roll-Ups and
pepperettes to dried fruit jerky that shook like a dead fish
and sheets of flatbread with goat cheese. Marcus would
rather go hungry, but was afraid to bring the food back
home since the only thing Frank ever said to him was,
"Do you really think you need seconds, son?" Gone also

133

were the occasional lunchbox notes on which his mother drew an eyeball followed by a fat heart followed by a giant capital U.

Marcus didn't get the chance to talk to his mother at supper anymore. Frank was busy telling her about the people he had helped throughout the day, about the elderly lady he had to carry to the examination table who asked him why he couldn't have been born fifty years earlier, but then, she said, he probably would have been shot in the war as all the handsome men were. And there was the young girl who came in for dialysis and was too shy to ever talk to anyone, but every visit she tugged on the sleeve of Frank's blue cotton scrubs and whispered that he was her favourite. Marcus wanted to storm into the hospital and show the old lady and the shy girl the kind of shit Frank was packing in his lunch.

By the time Marcus reached high school, he had slimmed down to what Frank considered an acceptable weight, and he'd somehow gotten over the dead fish texture of his dried fruit. The girls thought it was pretty cool that he ate hummus, liked the way he listened so well to their feelings, and the way his blond hair fell perfectly without his doing anything to it. He was still a little shy, but they didn't seem to mind. "You just get me," they all said.

Marcus's father, Niko, swung by the school about once every two months, unexpectedly, and took him out for lunch, which was fine because Mom and Frank wouldn't know, or for supper, which wasn't fine because Mom and Frank freaked out when Marcus wasn't home on time. He'd beg his dad to wait a few minutes so he could use the secretary's phone to call home, but Niko would run his hand against his agitated salt and pepper hair, wavy like his son's, and say, "Come on, Marcus—I want to get going. I'm a busy man, and I get to see you so rarely, I want to make the most of our time. Who's this pretty friend of yours?"

Marcus fumed the first time Niko spoke that way about whichever girl it was he happened to have at his side when his dad pulled his truck up along the curb in front of the school, but after he saw her face turn bright with a half fought-off smile, he understood his dad was showing him he cared, helping him out a little.

One of the pretty girls, Stephanie, asked Marcus if he wanted to hang out after school at her house, in her room, where she pulled his shirt off and ran her hands all over his back and her lips all over his face and told him she loved how gentle he was. Stephanie's dad had an electric guitar and started giving Marcus lessons. He had supper with her family a couple of times a week, and he watched as Stephanie and her sister bickered and laughed while mashing butter into potatoes, and as Stephanie repeated to her parents the stupid science joke her teacher had told. He thought about how it must feel to live with people who hear you.

"I feel like you like hanging out with my dad more than me," she said once as they walked along the ravine in her backyard. They had just returned from a drive into the city for a Blue Jays game, and Marcus had sat between

Stephanie and her dad, but had forgotten for most of it that she was there.

He didn't like her tone, the way it reminded him of his mom saying over and over again, "You could give Frank more of a chance," as if she were just making a suggestion.

"What the hell?" he said angrily, and turned red because he didn't know what else to say.

"I don't know," she started. "I mean, I know you're not close to your dad, and—"

"Just because I don't live with him doesn't mean we're not close. My dad just gets me, you know? No—maybe you wouldn't know." He stormed off back to her place, sat in the grey warmth of the basement, loudly strummed his five favourite chords and then left. After that he started to feel uncomfortable with her family, like maybe Stephanie had told her dad that Niko wasn't a great father, and wasn't Steph's dad trying too hard to be nice, and didn't the whole thing feel a little forced anyway.

Margot had been sitting beside him in choir. He told her she had a lovely voice, and she told him the same. He started taking the old guitar Niko had given him out at lunchtime and played "Free Falling" and "Summer of '69" for Margot. She thought he might like to come and play with her youth group sometime. The songs were easy to learn and the church smelled new to him despite its mustiness. He strummed the chords and watched Margot's elated face, her voice flirting around the notes as she asked God to wrap his arms around her, to hold her close forever. Playing with the band felt the way dinners at home should feel, the youth leader swinging his lead guitar against his gut and the rest of the teenagers spilling messy bright sounds around them.

The youth leader tried a little too hard to dumb down the bible stories, but Stan, the forty-year-old elder, who was balding and looked like the type to have a comb-over but didn't, was calm and kind. He took Marcus out for coffee one week and asked him what he thought about God, and Marcus said truthfully he hadn't given him much thought—the love and compassion thing sounded pretty good, but the stories were a little far-fetched. Stan lent Marcus the bible he had read as a teenager.

It was good timing because when he asked Margot why they couldn't get more physical, she told him to read his bible. She said it tenderly, with a promise behind it. So he started with Genesis and didn't find much about sex but found it pretty poetic, loved the word *void*, whispered it out loud before bed, the weight of the book bearing peacefully into his knees. "Then there was light," and he felt the warmth he felt when they prayed in the youth room surrounded by candles and standing lamps. The rest of Genesis started to get boring so he skipped over to the Psalms, where he loved the way David went rapidly from hope to despair. "That David was pretty emo," he told Margot one day. She smiled, and he felt she knew he was finally getting it.

The following year, having reached only second base, he was growing more excited about his spiritual life than about Margot. He loved sitting in the silence and listening to the thoughts in his head, trying to pull out the ones that were from God and the ones that might be from Satan. When he told Margot he needed to end things so he could focus on his faith, she smiled with both victory and pain. "Maybe it will work out again down the road, when we're both stronger," he said. With wet eyes she said, "I can't argue with God's will." He revelled in the relief that came with knowing she could love him, knowing he could hurt her with good intentions.

Stan met him for coffee a couple times a month, as often as Niko was supposed to see him, although Niko was swinging by unexpectedly only a few times a year now. Marcus told himself it didn't matter because he had Stan and his bible and the youth group, and praying was supposed to take the pain away. "And I'm so happy, so very happy—I've got the love of Jesus in my heart," he found himself humming through Frank's hospital stories at supper, finishing quickly so he could rush off to practise guitar. "What's most important," Stan emphasized, "more important than anything else in the world, is that you live according to Scripture." And if Stan lived this way, it could only mean good things. "There is no need to please man. If you follow what God tells you above all else, you can live life abundantly."

By the time Marcus was finishing high school, he had sworn off dating completely. There was no need to tie himself to one person, to be controlled by his physical desires. He liked the feeling of the girls' nearness when they swam in Stan's pool and played games with the girls perched on the guys' shoulders, their bare thighs wrapped around his neck. He liked the feeling of being so close and yet knowing he could keep them at bay, looking up from his guitar during youth group meetings and catching the eyes of a girl who was staring at him.

A week before he left for college, the youth group gathered around to pray over him, each person putting a hand on his arms, his shoulders. He tried to flex a little as girls wrapped their thin fingers around his arms. In that moment he knew the connectedness he felt had become something to live and die for. Jenny pulled a finger across his cheek to wipe his tears away. "You know we're all with you through prayer," she breathed in his ear. Stan promised to take him out for coffee every time he came home.

Frank drove Marcus to school, gave him a bike, looked his lean figure up and down and smiled at him with accomplishment. Marcus reached out to shake his hand before the man could hug him, but Frank pulled him in for one anyway, and the baby scent of his clean pressed scrubs stuck furiously in Marcus's nose all afternoon. His mother cried. "I've done the best I could, and you've turned out better than I could have asked for," she said with her hands wrapped around his cheeks.

Within the first week of school he was pining for the youth group. He bought orange printer paper and printed flyers to hang from any available bulletin board or telephone pole at the school:

LOOKING FOR SOMETHING MORE?
Find God's dreams for your life!
Weekly Bible study, time of worship, and fellowship.
Meets Mondays at 7:00 PM,
in the Denver Hall Common Area.
HOPE TO SEE YOU THERE!

He bought two bags of chips and bottles of no-name pop, picturing fifteen faceless bodies spread across the stiff couches and fold-out chairs in the common room, but forty people showed up to his first meeting, big-eyed and sitting on their hands, waiting for him to begin. He started by making a joke about God needing to miraculously multiply the snacks he brought, and everyone laughed a little, shyly, acceptingly. Like sheep without a shepherd, he thought, and felt overwhelmed with affection for these people he had just met.

Looking into their open faces, he deftly lifted Stan's bible into his lap and turned to the last place he had read. He cracked open the book and started talking about how much the word of God meant to him, about how badly they needed it in a world full of twisted truth and false love. One boy nodded faithfully at the end of each sentence. Marcus traded the bible for his guitar as he spoke and began strumming. A girl's eyes filled with tears. He began to sing, feeling the fullness of the tenor notes in his throat, his own sound washing over him. The evening turned into three hours, and at the end everyone stayed to talk long after the chip bags were empty. "This is exactly what I've been looking for," the bleary-eyed girl told him afterwards. He hugged her, smelled her lavender hair.

The group gained a few people each week, reaching a high of sixty-eight by exam season. Marcus loved how effortless it felt standing in front of everyone, filling the room with his voice. He would wake in the middle of the night, heart racing, and roll out of bed onto his knees to pray, to imagine all of the things he could say and ways he could inspire more intensity in his disciples. At the beginning of the second semester he announced that God was calling the group to meet twice a week.

Marcus, now going by Mark, felt the fire in his bones burning deeper and deeper each week and knew the rest of the group was feeling the same. They couldn't stand to be apart, couldn't wait to meet again, so he added another Friday-night meeting, since no one serious enough to be dedicated to the group was into partying anyway. By the time he added the Sunday-evening meeting and told them they need not feel bad for missing the watered-down services of the traditional churches they were dragging themselves out of bed for, the group had shrunk back down to a devoted thirty.

The Sunday sessions began with foot washing in the candle-lit common room, and because he couldn't do it all, Mark let Brandon, a slight boy with an uneven, quiet face, play sensitive worship songs softly while Mark started the washing. Round plastic tub in hand, towel around his waist, he would kneel, his blond curls hiding his angled cheeks as he bent his head over a girl's foot, massaging warm, sweet water into her sole, up the crest of her calf. Sometimes he started with a guy, to keep things balanced, but the guys welled up less often and left him feeling a little underwhelmed.

The use of the dormitory common area hadn't seemed to bother anyone until the all-night prayer vigils started every other week. The space filled with music, shouting, pacing, jumping, and all sorts of devoted activity that, according to Mark's RA, freaked the other residents out a little. "We want to make room for your religious expression, but this might be a little too intense for a public area." Mark knew discrimination could be expected when a group of people was committed to living passionately, but he still felt a little driven with righteous anger.

He found a church near the school with a congregation of ten white-haired people who were more than willing to rent the facility out four to five nights a week to young Christians at a meagre one hundred dollars a month. After Mark told the members of his group they needed to start paying rent and passed a bucket around during foot washing, he understood how much he was changing lives, how deep was their gratitude. The extra money could go towards important expenses that he was incurring. Having been so devoted to the group, he had neglected many of his own needs and desires and now God was rewarding him for his sacrifice.

"I KNOW THIS is all very exciting, Marcus," Stan said over coffee, having driven up to visit him, concerned he hadn't been home in so long, "but doesn't it seem a bit much? You're not getting rest, you aren't plugged into a bigger community—"

"Why would I need a bigger community? Who says bigger is better?"

"Well, I'm not saying it needs to be big, but I think you need some balance. I think you need some rest. You're doing so much work pouring into other people—who is pouring into you? Who's taking care of you, Mark?"

It was sweet that Stan worried, that he felt Mark should be provided for. Stan's words swept over Mark in a way that made him feel like dropping his head to the table and crying himself to sleep right then and there, in the safety of the old man's protective gaze.

But Mark had grown resistant to the attraction of rest. He patted Stan's bible, propped on the corner of the plastic table. "Right here. What else do I need?"

"Accountability, Marcus. You need to listen to other voices—"

And with that, a burning started in Mark's gut. "What other voices? No one else I know is living a life of true passion, a life of complete sacrifice to God." Marcus dipped the end of his pinky in the hot, black coffee, enjoyed the gentle burn he felt on his skin.

"I don't get it, Stan. I thought this is what you would want for me. I thought this was the point. You wanted me to be a leader. Now I am, having way more of an influence than I could have predicted. I thought you'd be happy." I thought you'd be proud, he thought.

Stan looked at him for a long enough time that Mark had to look away. He was searching for something in Marcus's eyes, something Mark wasn't ready for him to see. "Mark, aren't you lonely? Aren't you tired?"

"The joy of the Lord is my strength," said Mark. He thought about Stan, his gentle kindness and care. Was that enough? Wasn't this all about radical sacrifice, about giving up the self? After all these years of learning from Stan, it was time that Mark called Stan to account.

"I think this is one of those 'Get behind me, Satan' moments," Mark said. "You're trying to get me off the narrow path God has set before me."

Stan sighed, reached across the table and ran his index finger along the ridge of his bible, cracked with years of use. Mark felt a little sad about the way the tables had turned, the way he was so much more passionate than his wise old mentor, who had so much to learn from Mark now—if only he could be bothered to open his heart.

MARK'S CONVERSATION WITH Stan deepened his drive towards holiness, towards being set apart, unlike anyone else he knew. How easily he could have fallen for the devil's devices, dressed as a kind, older man, the one who had inspired Mark's faith the most over the years. How close he had come to falling for the seductive entice- ment to cool to lukewarm, the siren's call of "balance," "rest," or "self-care." These were words of the world that had no place in the life of devotion, and so Mark dedicated another hour of each day to prayer, waking at 4:00 AM to kneel at the side of his bed until his shins went numb.

He was a little annoyed with the way the dark circles growing under his eyes were changing his face, and more annoyed with his RA for mentioning that he looked exhausted every time he crossed his path. "You really should be getting more sleep," he told Mark, who replied, "I'll sleep when I'm dead."

"I don't get it," said the RA, shaking his head. "I just don't get what you're doing."

Mark put his hand on the RA's forearm. "I'm praying that one day you'll understand the passion I feel, what it means to live for more than comfort, what it means to have a spirit that drives you beyond human strength."

"Sure, but please don't pray for me while you should be sleeping," the RA said, rolling his eyes as he walked away. Mark had developed a tough skin against this sort of persecution, remembering that one day they would all understand: the guys in the dorm, Frank and Mom and Niko and even Stan—they would all know what they were missing.

The group dwindled to seventeen devoted members who kept up with the bi-weekly fasts and were willing to answer their phones for random 2:00 AM prayer walks around campus as the Spirit led, when Mark couldn't sleep. When the school year ended the white-haired congregants agreed to let the group rent out the entire church building to live in, with an arrangement that the students would take over the janitorial duties and grounds upkeep.

Only fourteen of the seventeen were willing to stay over the summer and move in together, and of those, two left after the first month. They waited in tear-stained shirts with their luggage on the curb for their older siblings to pick them up while the others yelled that they hoped they knew what they were leaving, that not everyone was ready to walk the narrow road. One girl's sister skidded up in front of the church, slammed the car door and yelled at Mark, "I could kill you for the way you've made my sister feel about herself! I hope you realize that you're ruining lives, and the rest of you," she threw her arm around above her head in angry circles, "should leave while you can."

"We can charge her with death threats," Marci said to Mark.

"In this life we will have trials," he said gently, "but I have overcome the world."

Mark watched the wayward followers slouch in their cars and drive away, and remembered that few were chosen. The group spent the summer gardening together, writing songs with Mark on guitar, plastering the walls of the nearly dead church with paintings of verses from Scripture or sayings Mark had invented and everyone quoted all the time, like "Love till it breaks you," and other poetry like "It's when you think you have nothing left that you are the strongest."

Stan continued to call every month or so, "Just checking in," as he would say in the cheery messages he left for Mark on the answering machine, "seeing how life is treating you." There was a sadness Mark could hear behind the cheeriness—or was it fear?—that reminded him of Frank's constant chiding about Mark's diet and weight. Mark avoided picking up the phone, knowing now that Stan's influence could only pull him away from his vision. And yet part of him longed for Stan to come and pick him up, the way the families of those who had left had. It wasn't that Mark wanted to go home. He wanted to be in the car, with Stan driving and navigating, and Mark could sit in the back seat, turn off his brain and watch the trees and billboards fly by.

In September Mark stopped wearing a watch. He felt free and naked without it, without Time holding him in place. The Spirit reminded him when he was supposed to go to class, if he was supposed to go, but often he skipped for more important things, like talking or bonding with the community over homemade lemonade. Every decision he made left him confident, flattered by divine guidance.

"You've been praying that God would make you beautiful, haven't you?" he asked Marci one day after individual prayer hour. She blushed a little. "Don't be ashamed," he said. "I can see it." He could hear the rest of the group laughing in the kitchen, and wondered why they were having so much fun without him, but knew he needed to be with her in that moment.

"I guess . . . I guess I've been longing for it my whole life. But it's only been in the last several months that I've been feeling it."

"That's what happens when you believe," he said, grasping her knee. He kissed her gaunt cheek, looked into her eyes, and left, feeling her gaze on him all the way out the door. He was so close to having her, and stronger for resisting every day. He had impressed upon them all that romance would distract from what they were called to do. But maybe he would change his mind, in a few years, when the others were strong enough.

In October, a writer for the student paper called and asked if he could stay with the group for a few days. "I'll have to pray about it and get back to you," Mark told him kindly. The following week, Andrew showed up with a sleeping bag and an air mattress, and the others, who had been toughing it out on the hard Sunday school floors, looked enviously at his fluffy bed, but Mark insisted living for God wasn't comfortable; why did they need beds when Jacob used a rock for a pillow and the son of God had no place to lay his head?

Andrew sat quietly in the corner during worship time, talked for hours with Mark about music, joined in their massage lines and scribbled happily in his notebook during foot-washing.

"So what inspired you to do this whole thing you're doing here?" Andrew asked after one late-night worship service. Everyone else had gone to bed.

"Life's too easy," Mark said with heavy eyes. He was tired and wanted to sleep, but he liked Andrew's curiosity, wanted to honour it. "We're coddled in our society. We want everything to be comfortable. But Jesus calls us to challenge ourselves, to be different than everyone else. If we accept that call, we get jolted out of our day-to-day existence. We connect with each other, with ourselves, on a deeper level."

"Reminds me a bit of mountain climbing," Andrew said. "Life here, in the city, starts to wear on you. I start to feel like my soul is empty. Until I'm up on a rock face, and then I feel like I'm connected with everyone and everything, the way it pulls me out of the monotonous, reminds me there's more to life."

"Yeah, exactly!" Mark said.

"And then I come back home," Andrew said, "and it's like I'm walking around with the blinders off and no one else gets it."

"Yep," said Mark. "That's God trying to get your attention."

"Ha—maybe," said Andrew. "Maybe."

They talked for another couple of hours, Mark in his exhaustion drifting off into a trance-like state, letting the words flow from him with little attention to what he said. Andrew seemed rapt with Mark's words, in a way the group used to be, before they had grown lazy of listening. Mark woke up the next morning with his head resting on Andrew's air mattress, Andrew's sleeping bag draped over him.

Andrew seemed at home with the group, and Mark delighted in watching their hospitality. He wondered if the article might lead more people to make this pilgrimage, if their numbers might increase again and revival might break out now that people would know the kind of radical love the group shared. Every night after the group wrapped up, Andrew and Mark stayed up, jamming on the guitars, reflecting on how few opportunities there are in life for true highs, for true deep connection. At the end of the week, Mark was surprised when Andrew reached out his hand and said, "I guess my time here has wrapped up. This has been great." Mark pulled him into a hug, and Andrew leaned in.

"Please don't be a stranger," Mark said, and he felt a heaviness in his chest, heavier than when the backsliders had left the group earlier that summer. "You belong here," he said. Then he handed Andrew Stan's bible, believing he could sense the preciousness of the gift.

Two weeks after Andrew left, the dean of students emailed Mark to come in for an appointment in his office. As Mark settled his thin buttocks in the soft peach chair, the dean leaned forward, his forearms pressed along the centre of the desk, hands clasped in front of him, and said, "I'm just going to come out and ask the obvious: what do you make of these rumours that you're running a cult?"

Mark laughed out loud. He laughed so hard his stomach hurt, his eyes watered, and the dean had to look away uncomfortably. Something about the dean's tone, gentle and concerned, reminded Marcus of his coffee with Stan. "Why," asked Mark, gasping, "how—who thinks we're a cult?"

"You haven't seen the paper?" the dean asked. He pushed it across the table to Mark. His eyes grew wet as he ran them along the tiny black print, scanning for key words: *love, kindness, cult, high, countercultural.*

"This is ridiculous. The guy had a great time—he had a great time. Look—see here? He says 'undeniably the kindest people you'll ever meet.' He's just trying to publish a crazy story for shock value—get a lot of publicity for the paper."

"Marcus, everyone in the group is doing poorly in school, some are on academic probation, some failing courses. You're only enrolled in three courses and failing two of them. I want to be upfront about it with you, as you're adults and all. But when parents are funding their children's education, I need to inform them when I'm this concerned about their academic, and general, well-being." He breathed deeply.

"That's all, Marcus. That's all."

A WEEK LATER, Marci's parents showed up and insisted on taking Mark out for coffee. As Mark fervently stirred a stream of sugar into his mug, Marci's dad began.

"We wanted to meet with you because we appreciate what you guys have been trying to do." He used Frank's "have a salad instead" tone of voice, intentionally generous, the one that insisted things were going to change. "We know you're all adults and we've wanted to give Marci the freedom to be a part of this experiment. But we've become quite concerned. She's distant, and we can see that she's exhausted—"

"Well, I understand it's tempting to think life shouldn't be challenging, but we need to show the world that things can be different."

"She's not happy, Mark," Marci's mom said.

"Happy? What would you know about happiness? She's told me she's never been more fulfilled in her life! You just can't tell because it's a different kind of happiness than you've ever been able to offer her—"

"It's clear that I can't change your mind, son," said the father loudly, and Mark flinched a little in his seat, "but we need to tell you we're taking Marci home with us."

"Well, I think that's Marci's choice, isn't it?"

"It is and she's made it. She was scared to talk to you about it, and quite frankly, I can see why. She's packing up now, and we'll come by again this evening to pick her up."

Mark didn't have much else to say.

AFTER MARCI'S PARENTS dropped him off, he seethed down the hallway and stood in her doorway, hands pressed on both sides of the doorframe. She was pulling down hand-painted posters of bible verses—PERFECT LOVE DRIVES OUT ALL FEAR, one said in Marci's rounded letters, with heart-shaped O's.

"You're invaluable here," he said as he stepped into her room. "We can't keep being who we are without you. You belong with us. Don't you know how much you mean to me?" He wrapped his arms around her, pressing his chest tight against hers.

"I know, I know—I'm sorry," she sobbed, and her aggravating tears soaked through his T-shirt. "I'll come back," she said as he pulled away from her. "I just need a break for a bit—"

"Marci, that's not how commitment works!" he shrieked. Her eyes went wide. He wanted to slap them shut. "You're in it or you're not! I guess living radically got too hard for you, and the Enemy has cushier shit to offer you! So go, Marci! But you can't come crawling back when you have enough money but you feel so damn empty that life isn't worth living anymore!"

He slammed the door as she wailed on. It was for the best, he thought, while his pulse raced, his head throbbing.

Mark walked slowly down the hall, dragging his fingers along the walls, towards the music wafting from the living room. He could hear the phone ringing at him from another room, their landline, the one invasion from the outside world. He now realized it had been ringing throughout his conversation with Marci. He thought it might be Frank or Mom, or maybe Niko, none of whom had offered to visit, to meet "the kindest people you'll ever meet," see what he was capable of making. Maybe it was Andrew, realizing what he was missing, calling to say that he was finally accepting that the high he chased up those mountains could be with him all the time. Over the phone's buzz, in his mind he heard Frank's voice—"Marcus, could you get off the couch for once and answer the phone?" He sent Frank's voice and the ringing phone and Marci away to the place in his mind where he sent all of the people who tried to pull him away from his vision—his RA, Stan, the dean, Andrew. He walked away from the ringing, towards the music. He stood outside the living room door, the bold fluorescent light of the hallway shining around him against the dimness of the candle-lit living room.

Brandon was playing a hymn softly on his guitar. It bothered Mark, Brandon playing so often, almost more than Mark, but he could talk to him about his spirit of arrogance later. Some were prostrate on the floor, curled inward as fetuses, a few were swaying with eyes half closed, half leaning against the walls. Mark stepped in, and the lamp shook as he began to jump up and down. He threw his head back for the last line of the song. "And now I am happy all the time," he screamed.

MATTRESS SURFING

BODIES JOSTLE AND SETTLE INTO place on the silky mattress plunked in the middle of the gravel driveway. Like some kind of failed orgy, Emily thinks, her skin bristling against the pink evening air. She stands watching while the rest shimmy around for the best spots—the women clamber for safety in the centre, and then men plunk themselves down along the edges, beer bottles nestled in their elbow crooks. They laugh and shove and link arms like a game of Red Rover–meets–Sardines.

"Come on, Emily!" the balloon pilot calls as if she were a mile away, waving his arm wildly above his head. She

155

looks towards the farmhouse, and around the red barns behind them, trying to invent an excuse to avoid wedging herself into the mix of sweat and beer breath. She relents and shuffles onto the edge of the mattress where the pilot is perched, giving him the opportunity to reach an arm around her protectively. He doesn't.

"Have you been mattress surfing before?" he asks.

"Can't say I have."

A girl beside him leans too close and says, "He invented it," tapping her plastic wine goblet against the pilot's chest. "Always the adventurous one."

The pilot's bearded cheeks rise with his smile. "It's become a tradition," he says. "Every time someone needs to get rid of a mattress, I guess. Started in high school when Jenny's mom moved in with her new boyfriend and Jenny had to go with her. Kirkby picked the mattress up with his truck and hooked it up to the tractor, and we all piled on and drove along Dingman's Lane. And then, when James moved in with his girlfriend and graduated from his twin bed, we had to pile on top of each other to all fit!" He exhales a chesty laugh. The girls beside him echo with drunk giggles.

"This one's Kirkby's," the pilot says. "His wife just left him."

Kirkby is hunched over the front of the mattress, stabbing it with a large hook on the end of a chain linked to a small tractor. He struggles to tear through the silky fabric that holds the springs and stuffing and other mattress innards intact.

A puff of orange stretches above the alfalfa fields. Emily is drunker than she should be at a party this early in the evening. She still feels out of place around the pilot's friends. It's clear they all think she is lucky to be with him, and she is beginning to fear she doesn't feel the same.

They met two months ago at a stag and doe. She asked how he got into the air balloon business and he said he "started on the ground crew in high school—one of the guys who follows the balloon in the car and has to guess where it'll land. Then you run up and anchor it. You have to jump on it while it's still sort of dragging on the ground, add your weight to it." He used his hands to demonstrate, one sweeping across the sticky table heel first, the other making a person out of two finger legs running across and then lunging at the basket.

When she told him she was a prenatal ultrasound tech, he said, "Whoa. That must be empowering. To help people see right inside themselves. To be there for one of the most intimate moments in someone's life." He took a sip and looked at the counter fondly. "That's meaningful work."

She pulled at the itchy collar of her shirt. "There's a lot of gross stuff, and technical stuff. Most of it isn't that interesting."

"Lots of technical stuff in my work, too. Waivers and driving, cleaning and repairs—but all worth it when you see the joy on people's faces. You must know that feeling." He perked up in an epiphany, a reaction Emily has come to expect every few minutes in their conversations. "Hey, what you and I do is not that different! We help people see themselves from different perspectives, to see the world in a way you can't on your own." She thought this was sweet, self-aware cheesiness.

At first it was endearing, the cartoonishness of his career and his passion, but it's beginning to wear on her, the way he refers to himself as a "pilot, but not the traditional kind," the same rehearsed story to answer the inevitable questions about how he got into such an interesting line of work. Besides, he seldom initiates anything physical. And she is losing hope that he will take her up into the air for a ride.

She has imagined it more times that she cares to admit, the heat of the flame against their faces, how the balloon would catch boisterously in the wind and she would fall against him, and he would catch her and kiss her, pressing her against the edge of the basket, the land two hundred empty feet below.

But he's mentioned several times that they are booked solid all summer. And four out of five days they have to cancel, due to any amount of wind or rain or fog, or if the fields are too wet. "It's my job to protect the passengers," he said once. "So if that means they want to yell at me because they're not getting the ride they want, that's okay. I'd rather that than anyone be hurt."

"So essentially it has to be a perfect day for you to go," she said.

"Pretty much."

"Sounds like a scam."

"It does," he said, "until you get up there."

Somehow this line gave her goose pimples in a way that felt like self-betrayal. She wondered if the same were true of his affection, that he did not show it until he considered the moment perfect, all the elements aligned in a way that neither of them could control.

Kirkby finally breaks through the mattress and secures it with the hook. He jumps into the tractor, which growls and blows warm exhaust onto the passengers. Kirkby grins back at them, and Emily tries frantically to get a grip on the corner of the mattress.

The tractor pulls the chain taut so the mattress jolts into entertainment mode. "Yee-haw!" calls one of the guys at the back, and the girls in the middle giggle. Dirt and gravel are spitting up into Emily's eyes and nose. She takes a deep breath and breaks into a coughing fit as her throat and lungs fill with dust.

"Don't breathe through your mouth!" the pilot yells.

THAT AFTERNOON AT work the doctor had been called away from the clinic, which made Emily anxious because it meant she had to continue through failed pregnancies as if nothing had happened, remaining aloof to the patients' questions until a medical professional could follow up with a proper diagnosis.

Emily had greeted a woman who brought that palpable joy of pregnancy to the dimly lit room. Emily seldom shared the excitement anymore, finding a detached presence more beneficial for both herself and the patient. There had just been too many disappointments.

This woman was bigger than she should be for ten weeks, her tight T-shirt bulging a little at the belly.

Emily ran through her rehearsed lines: "Could you lift up your shirt for me, please?" and "I'm going to apply the gel to your stomach now. It might be a little cold."

"I've been trying for two years now," the woman said, reaching up to touch the gauzy orange fabric around her neck. The scarf was swallowed up in the ridges of her neck as she leaned forward to watch the wand roll around on her belly, pushing out secrets of new life into the machine. But Emily could see that there was no life inside her, only lesions growing all along the inside of her uterus.

"Can you see it?" the woman asked.

"Not right now," said Emily distantly. She dragged the probe along, driving waves of sound through the cancer, reflected brightly onto her screen. She wanted to say, "Don't you know? Can't you feel inside yourself that things are not right?" And yet, she thought, the signs can all be wrong—presumably this cancer had provided the woman with a false positive on her pregnancy tests.

After one sharp prod from Emily's transducer, the woman's hand shot up protectively to her gel-covered belly—misdirected maternal instincts firing off. Emily turned the screen away from the woman's arching neck, refusing to look at her. But the orange scarf kept flickering in the corner of her vision.

"I'm supposed to be able to see it," the scarf said. "The doctor said I could."

"Usually you can," Emily said, trying to keep the

transducer in her hand from shaking, "but I'm having some difficulties with the monitor."

Emily knew the woman feared what she thought was the worst, though she did not know what the worst was. After a minute the scarf asked quietly, "Did I miscarry?"

"No," said Emily, which was true, as there had never been anything there to miscarry. But everything within her tightened as soon as she said it, as if someone had wrapped elastics around every joint and muscle.

The woman's fist clenched and unclenched around the ends of the scarf. Emily pressed the wand into the wrong answers. She dug around, trying to get the clearest images of lumps and growths reverberating through the woman's uterus that, at best, would mean she would survive and never bear the child she wanted.

"I'VE LANDED IN this field before," says the pilot, leaning his mouth close to her ear and pointing as they ride. She tries to look up, but immediately her eyes sting with dirt and resentment.

"Right there, close to the road." His voice rattles over the gravel. "We dragged for a while through the crops. Kirkby's dad wasn't too happy that we took out some of his plants."

Kirkby turns smoothly onto the road, and the mattress follows obediently. He turns and screams out of the window, "Damn you, Paula! Damn you and the mattress you fucked around on!"

The riders holler and yelp back, beer glasses clinking with cheers. Kirkby's tractor jolts into third gear.

Kirkby begins to yank the tractor wheel back and forth. The mattress fishtails and its occupants lean to and fro, with exaggerated whoops and giggles. The mass of friends suddenly lurches too hard against Emily, and she tumbles through the gravel, then rolls into the tall grass on the shoulder.

She lies there a minute, closing her eyes against the pain and whirling dust, waiting for the sound of the tractor turning around to come back for her. It doesn't.

She rubs pebbles from her arm. Her arm holds the memory of the pilot trying to grab her and hold her on, but the jolt must have been too hard.

Her entire left side stings. The crickets buzz in unison with her pain. Then she realizes that all of the tiny elastics wrapped around her have snapped. She wraps her throbbing arm around her throbbing knees.

Footsteps skim the gravel behind her, coming closer. She runs her fingers along her grimy cheek. She wants to be angry at him, but she isn't. She wants to remember the reason she picked him. His hand is on her bruised shoulder, his toes against her behind. He bends over above her, his face upside-down.

"Scraped up bad, eh?" he says to the top of her head. She nods. The skin on her reddening leg pulses as he comes around to face her, takes off his grubby T-shirt. His beard is grey with dust in contrast to the protected fuzz on his chest. He wraps the shirt around her leg. It's an odd romantic gesture, and she grins as he gently ties the sleeves in a knot.

He pulls her into his bare chest, a miscalculated hug in which her face is pressed against his armpit. He runs his hand up and down her back. He offers a comfort she hasn't earned, a comfort she wishes she could send through the air to the scarf.

They sit in silence for a few minutes, watching the sun give off a last glow.

"Do you know," he asks quietly, "why they always serve champagne after a balloon ride landing?"

She shakes her head.

He leans back on his elbows, unconcerned with the dew. "Back when they were first invented, people were pretty religious, superstitious. You know that whole, 'If God meant men to fly he would have given them wings' type thing."

She knows he has told this story again and again, rehearsed and unoriginal. And yet she wants to hear it so badly, to be part of his floating world, even if it's happening in the wrong order.

"So the first guys to make an air balloon crashed it in a farmer's field and proceeded to light the farmer's field on fire. The farmers run out to the balloon, convinced that it's the devil's work, ready to run them through with their pitchforks. Then the balloon pilots pull out their champagne. In those days only the nobles were allowed to drink it, so when they offered it to the peasants, obviously they had to be from the nobility and the nobility had been put in place by God, so it must be good."

He sighs. "Now it seems the farmers are still ready to run you through with pitchforks for damaging their crops.

The champagne doesn't make up for it. There was a time when you'd be welcomed like a celebrity."

He leans over her, reaching out to her with a practised arm. And somehow for the first time, the rehearsed aspect of his lines and gestures make the whole process more meaningful, like all the previous times had been in preparation for this moment. He does not know it yet, but this might only go on another day or month or two, and then it will pass, and Emily and the pilot will simply be memories for each other. The woman will know her bad news by then, will have her uterus pulled up from her body, and with it, her core hopes. But other news will also come and go, bad and good.

The pilot gently wraps one arm around her, runs the other hand through her tangled hair. The tractor is coming back around and its rumble is growing, the headlights flickering against Emily's eyelids as it bumps along the gravel. Its squeaky honk drowns out the buzz of the insects. She and the pilot laugh as the friends on the broken-marriage mattress slide by and catcall to them, their voices a brief stream of sound through the dusky air, and then just an echo as they float away.

ROAD PIZZA

O N THEIR WAY BACK FROM the Beer Store, the night before the accident, Volk and Jason found the road pizza. The car's headlights along the causeway lit up the white pizza box, and they pulled over to find a fully intact Hawaiian pizza.

When they got back to the cottage, they folded pieces together and ate them like sandwiches. Rachel and I wouldn't touch the stuff.

"Seriously, best pizza ever," Jason said with pride as we brushed our teeth before bed.

"Don't kiss me," I heard Rachel shriek at Volk from

their bedroom. "Who knows where that pizza's been."

The next morning, the Saturday before Labour Day, Jason and Volk sat shirtless on the second-storey deck drinking breakfast beers. Rachel and I sat below them at the dock in wraparound skirts and bikinis. The fish in the channel bobbed and opened their tiny grey mouths like a nursery of babies learning to coo.

"Can't be good for them, all these carbs," said Rachel, tossing stale sour cream and onion chips to the fish.

"There's that turtle," Jason called down from above us, pointing a sloshing beer towards the water. The turtle poked his sharp face out of the water amongst the fish, pretending to belong.

"I swear that's the one we saved," he said. He had been quite proud of himself last summer when he spotted the little thing crossing the causeway, the wetness of its shell gleaming. He pulled the car over and lifted the small creature into the trunk. When we arrived at the cottage he carried it safely to the channel.

If it was the same one, it was now three times the size, and would frequently sun on the banks of the channel. "He's thanking us," Jason said, leaning over the edge of the wooden railing, "by entertaining us."

"You're blocking my sun," I called back to him.

That day last summer when he found the turtle was when Jason and I hooked up for the first time, in the musty air of the boathouse. We lay on a deflated inner-tube on the cement floor, the water lapping against the boat rhythmically, encouragingly. Rachel and Volk had started dating at the end of first year and had been together three months. "Jason's so sweet," Rachel would say when we were alone, "and cute," prodding me in the ribs with a dainty elbow. But I had resisted, looking for more of a reason to be with him than the expectations of friends.

When we returned to school after the summer I was unsure of what to make of things with Jason. It was convenient and comforting, the four of us going to the Strange Wolf in the evenings, cramming together on a tattered couch in Volk and Jason's apartment to watch movies, Rachel and I huddled under a blanket at the boys' rugby games. But during our weekends at Volk's cottage, it seemed we could spend a lifetime together and never grow tired of each other.

Across the channel two kids were trying to start a fire from the embers in their fire pit, still flickering from the night before. They prodded the coals with dried pine branches till they smoked, pulled them out, stared at the red glow pulsing through orange needles, shrieking at the power smouldering in their hands.

Volk and Jason finished their beers and their conversation evolved into wrestling. Rachel and I closed our eyes behind sunglasses, listening to the wooden balcony creak with the tension of two bodies jostling on its two-by-four flooring, huffing and laughing and cursing, boys wrapping their arms around each other in false aggression.

With a hard shove from Jason, three stakes of pine lining the space between the railing and the deck's floor gave way against Volk's weight and released him to the grass.

He didn't yell. Had he not fallen backwards the damage would have been a shattered ankle or a kneecap driven down against his shin. But when we reached him, his eyes were closed, his head sharply twisted, chin pressed against his bare shoulder. Rachel passed out and fell against me. The kids from across the channel screamed behind us. Jason grabbed the railing above the jagged hole where Volk had broken through.

"Volk, come on, you bastard!" he yelled, his eyes pinched in panicked laughter. "You bastard—you're fine, damn it!" He was still up there when Rachel came to and the ambulance arrived. I helped her into the passenger seat of her car and then jumped in the driver's seat to follow it to the hospital.

"Should we grab him a shirt?" Rachel asked as I turned the ignition.

When we came back that night to pack up our stuff and tell Jason that Volk was in good spirits but probably wouldn't walk again, Jason was gone.

When classes started again in September, I sat down with Rachel to schedule breaks between our classes to visit Volk in the hospital. I called her every evening. I called Jason as well to invite him to join us, but he never picked up and I never left messages. I gave him his space for the first week and then swung by their apartment. The lights were off and no one came to the door. I walked by the field during rugby practice a few times. My heart stopped when I saw Volk's number on the back of a jersey moving along the field, but then I realized the player's hair was brown, not blond.

The first few weeks Rachel stayed dry-eyed during our visits, eating the cubes of blue Jell-O Volk got with his dinner tray, filling him in on what was going in our classes.

She'd let it all out on the way back. She started calling Volk by his first name. "Ryan's just so calm," she would say, saying the *Ry* part in a high-pitched tone, like she was talking to a baby. "Ryan's so calm, I feel like I'm holding all his grief."

Volk asked about Jason from time to time, turning to me for the answers. "He's good!" I'd say, overly chipper. Then worried about making him seem insensitive, I'd say, "He's having a hard time with things."

"Yeah. So am I." Volk turned away, and Rachel squeezed his hand.

"Did I tell you Aleesa Prins is pregnant?" she asked.

"Bet she's still hot," Volk said, a smile returning to his face. Rachel fake punched him playfully in the shoulder.

"Not fair," he said. "I can't fight back."

One time on the drive home Rachel said, "I think you should apologize. On Jason's behalf."

I was quiet for a minute. "Why should I do that?"

"Volk needs an apology, for closure. You're closest to Jason."

"That's not my job. And he knows Jason is sorry."

"I'm not sure any of us knows how Jason feels. He's been taking the easy way out."

"That's not fair. Besides, I don't even know if he's still in school."

"You could try harder. You could fight for the relationship."

We didn't talk for the rest of the ride. I dropped Rachel off at her dorm without saying a word.

"I sometimes think it's amazing," said Volk one time during that half year of visits, "that we didn't get sick from that pizza." Rachel laughed generously, the way you laugh on a first date. "It couldn't have been there too long," I said, "or the raccoons would have gotten it."

"But why was it there?" Volk asked. "Maybe someone pissed on it. Maybe a couple was fighting in their car and one of them threw it out the window. 'I told you no pineapple!' kinda thing. Or the pizza delivery guy got a fake order and threw it away. Maybe someone licked it and threw it out 'cause they thought it tasted like ass."

"Did it?"

"Can't remember. We were too excited about free food to care. I think what happened," Volk said, "was someone put the pizza on top of their car while they unlocked it, or while they made out in the parking lot, or something. They just forgot it was there and drove off." He knew the other reasons were more interesting, but this was the most likely.

Rachel eventually stopped picking up my calls as well. "I just want more time alone with *Ryan*," she told me finally. After that we would pass each other on campus and she would hug me without looking at me, would tell me it had been too long (I know, really too long!) and we needed to do coffee (yeah, that would be great!) or something soon, but she was in a rush (of course, so am I), so she'd call me soon, honey, smooch, miss you (miss you too).

A few months after the accident, once the family had accepted Volk's paralysis, Volk's dad tried to sue the builder of the cottage, who turned the blame to the architect. After a year of periodic court dates, Volk in his wheelchair at each one, the architect had his licence revoked and Volk had a settlement, the details of which he wouldn't explain. Volk went back to school the following year, graduated and went to law school last I heard.

The following spring I got drunk on a first date and told the guy about the balcony. I think I must have laughed when I told him, though I don't remember the telling, only his response.

"Wow," he said. "Wow. Guys, eh? I read on Yahoo news about a guy whose friends poured lighter fluid over his crotch when he fell asleep at a party, and lit his pants. Just thought it was funny—they'd do it to each other's socks all the time. The fire went out of control, second degree burns all over his, you know. He sued his best friends, and the parents. They settled."

When he drove me home after dinner, I threw up out the window. I watched the vomit spread out like long fingers across the side of his car.

The next day I rented a car and drove two hours to visit the cottage. I called Rachel one last time to ask if she wanted to come with me.

"That's weird," she said. "I think you need to let it go."

"Okay, thanks for weighing in," I said.

She told me she was thinking of breaking up with Ryan. "We don't really have anything in common anymore. Honestly, I think I've just stayed with him because he needed me. But we've moved past that."

"I think you have too," I said.

She told me a friend had said Jason quit school and moved into his parents' basement. He was taking courses online. He had gained a lot of weight, "about a hundred pounds. He hasn't been very active. He feels bad about the whole thing," the friend had told her. "And he misses you," Rachel said.

Months earlier I would have asked about a way to contact him. But "I miss him too," was all I could say. And "I hope he's doing alright."

The cottage looked as it should, dark and empty and in need of a good paint. In the back the balcony was still broken, the jagged stumps of posts pointing towards the clouds.

When I opened the door to the boathouse, a raccoon hobbled towards me and hissed. I could hear her kits whimpering from some unknown place.

I sat on the dock and threw bits of cracker into the water. After a few minutes the grey fish gathered and bopped around below me, but it was the turtle I wanted to see.

I ran out of cracker crumbs and so I took to throwing tiny stones from the garden. It was cruel to trick the fish this way but I needed to keep them searching to draw out the turtle.

After an hour I gave up. Perhaps he had abandoned this place with us no longer here to entertain. Perhaps he had tried to cross the causeway again and had not encountered a vehicle kind enough to pull over.

THE WHOLE BEAUTIFUL WORLD

"FUCK YOU, TEDDY BEAR," GEORGE says quietly, pointing to the centre of his blankets piled on the floor. His normally slurred speech is crisp with consonants. I'm helping him make his bed as I do most days. It's a slow process that consists of my asking questions like, "What do we do next, George?" and "Where do your pillows go?" He usually mumbles about something unrelated while I encourage him to join me in picking up blankets and spreading them across his train-track bedsheets.

"What do you want to wear today, dude?" I ask. Often he'll give me an up-down with his eyes and then base his decision on what I'm wearing. "Shorts," he says today. I guess he trusts my assessment of the weather. "Stripes,"

"What've you got against Teddy Bear?" I ask, pulling a pair of shorts from the dresser drawer. He doesn't have any stripes, but plaid will do.

"I don't know why Teddy Bear is so upset," he says. "I tell him, Teddy Bear, watch your mouth, Teddy Bear."

I haven't been correcting George on his swearing lately, even though we're supposed to find ways of "redirecting his language." But his speech impediment makes it difficult for strangers to discern what he says, and don't we all have the right to say what we want in our own bedrooms?

I've made this argument to the other home-care workers, who nod with understanding smiles and then say, "But Marty, George doesn't always know the difference between private space and shared space."

"I think George knows a lot more than he lets on," I'll say. It's a bit of an unfair response as we all know it's true, not only for George but for many of the members of Maison de la Paix. And no one can argue as I spend more time with George than anyone.

Most days George doesn't talk like this. Most days he'll stop and say, "I love you," and put a hand on your arm, smile at you with that smile he and his mother share when they sit together on the porch swing after her suppertime visits, her cradling his face in her hands. This is appropriate behaviour, the kind we are supposed to affirm, unlike hugs, which can be unpredictable, which can turn into a headlock without warning. Despite the fact that he does little to stay active, I'm guessing I'm the only person in the home who can match his strength. I'm guessing because I've never had to test it.

It's mostly his parents who are upset by his swearing. He hasn't learned it from us, and he certainly didn't learn it from them. His brother Bill who visits from time to time says George picked up his colourful vocabulary during his half year of Grade 10. He was energetic as ever and was getting too big for his mother to care for him. The principal assured her the high school had all the resources to "make the necessary accommodations for people like him." George had a good first month, despite picking up a bit of foul language, until a boy in his special needs class eyed his bright train-engine pencil and grabbed it out of George's hand. George stood up and pulled him into a strangling headlock, the boy's face bulging and purple, his tiny hands reaching up and clawing at George's pale forearm until it bled.

The educational assistants managed to set the boy free, still cradling the broken pencil in his hands. They pinned George face-first to the ground, hands clasped behind his back, chanting their mantras of "It's alright, George. Everything's going to be fine, George," while he kicked and cursed. "Fucking enemy! Fucking Satan!" "Mainstream students" gathered around in the hallway, listening and taking turns peeking through the doorway, frightened and entertained.

When the police arrived George's pained anger turned to uncontrollable excitement: he's always loved people in uniform.

"Policeman! Policeman!" he screamed with joy, banging his knees against the floor, his bleeding arm still pinned by the chanting EAs. The police reached for their tasers, as police do when confused. Fortunately George had already begun to hyperventilate and passed out before his heroes could jolt his body into submission.

His father had been out in the field and his mother, who spoke mostly Low German, couldn't understand what the secretary was saying until she got to the word *hospital*. She ran out to the field to get George's father, and they drove up together, not knowing what to expect.

When they arrived at his room, he was sedated, lying happily in a white bed with a fluffy blue teddy bear hanging from his bandaged arm. In the ensuing weeks he would pick the scabs, leaving himself with scattered scars and patches where his arm hair refused to grow back.

I didn't know him at the time, but I imagine George greeting his parents with his first ever drugged smile as they walk in and are introduced to this half-present version of him. It's a smile I've seen from time to time after he's had an aggressive episode or when his psychologist experiments with his concoctions of pills. Often after a vicious spell, when a housemate has been hit or a volunteer announces she won't be coming back, one of the home-care workers suggests we revisit his meds. The new treatments leave him as peaceful as can be, but virtually lifeless, sleeping fifteen hours a day, or roaming around with a pasty smile and blank eyes, touching the wallpaper trains in his room. Drugged, he is disinterested in his colouring books or building blocks or anything else.

"He's not happy when he's violent and angry all the time," a worker will say.

"But he also doesn't want to sleep all day," someone will respond.

"He deserves to live in peace."

And we'll debate together the best way of life for him, what each of us thinks he wants, or what we want him to want.

What's better, to be victim to your own strength and emotions, or to not even know what they are?

While he was growing up, George's parents determined that he had enough challenges communicating with society without trying to fight through two languages. So even though George's father and five siblings switched gracefully between Low German, Spanish, and English, when George began to speak at age three the older children and their father strictly limited their conversations to English. This meant George had few words to share with his mother; as a stay-at-home Old Colony Mennonite she never felt it necessary to become fluent in English. I guess it also meant that, for George's sake, conversation between his mother and the rest of the family was strained.

"For George's sake," is a phrase his brother Bill uses from time to time, laced with affection and resentment. "Our parents caved and finally got a TV, for George's sake." "We couldn't go camping, for George's sake." "Mom stopped working at the bakery and stayed home, for George's sake."

For George's sake they moved him into Maison de la

Paix, Bill told us. But we know it was more for his mother's sake. One afternoon a few months after he was kicked out of high school, when he had grown to his full height of six feet, his mother scolded him for tearing all the carrots out of the garden prematurely. He wrapped her in a frustrated hug so tight he broke two of her ribs.

She'd hobbled out back to the field to get George's father, who stormed back to find George sitting on the front porch, rocking quietly, Teddy Bear in hand. His father slapped him so hard that George fell off the porch onto the cement walkway.

I don't know this part for sure. I only know that he had two skinned knees and the handprint still on his cheek when he moved into the home.

We found out from his brother that George's mother was distraught about him leaving, and not too thrilled about him joining a Catholic group home. But she had little say in either matter, and as his father said, "Catholic is better than heathen." He had been ready to send George to a state-run home, but spending a little extra on a Christian organization was his way of making peace with his wife after his very unpacifist impulse.

George's brother Bill claims he had never been violent at home before that episode. Of course the event corresponded with his finishing puberty, a time when boys with brain injuries often become more physical and violent. And of course, it's possible he hit his mother from time to time before that and she never told anyone for fear that she would lose him.

Still, she only visits once a month. Some of the staff think she's guilt-ridden about George having to live without her. Others think George's dad is afraid of him hurting her again, and, because she doesn't have her licence, she can't come without him.

"Fuck off, Teddy Bear," George says again, pointing angrily to the matted bear now perched on top of his pillow. I've been scurrying around trying to throw his Lego into the bin. We're supposed to do his chores together, me empowering him to take care of himself, which I fully and wholeheartedly agree is the way to do things; however, we've been trying to get ready for an hour already and he's still wearing the train-engine pajama top.

"Which shirt?" I say, waving my hand towards the open drawer.

George reaches across me towards the tie-dyed shirt that says, JAMAICAN ME CRAZY! In the process he scuffs my arms with his long fingernails. George doesn't like his nails being cut, and doesn't have the dexterity to do it himself without clipping off slivers of flesh. The clicking, the cutting of something from his body, puts him on edge. I'm the only one who can do it without getting swatted, but I have to wait for the right moment, and given he's been pretty hard on Teddy Bear this morning, I'm not sure today is the day.

I'm not sure exactly why George is the way he is—some sort of complication during birth, the umbilical cord tied around his neck when he was born, that caused a severe lack of oxygen, something the doctors should have caught earlier, and most parents would have sued over. But the family concluded "It is the Lord's will," and "What we often consider curses are the greatest blessings." I guess if I had been raised in a family like that, I'd be saying, "Fuck you" to the teddy bear too, to anything that had ears.

George pulls the T-shirt over his head without taking off his pajama top. I let him struggle for a bit, hoping he'll figure it out. It's an odd dance, letting him do life, make mistakes, trying to weigh when to step in and when to let him fight.

"George," I blurt out after a few seconds, "let's take your PJs off first."

By now he is agitated, his hands wound together in the T-shirt fabric bundled above and around his head. I've let it go on too long.

"Can I help you?" I say. I take his mumbling "fucking enemy shirt" as a yes, and try to pull the cloth over his hands. He has begun swinging his arms around wildly. I duck to avoid being pummelled. I begin to sing softly in my low bass, "He's got the whole wo-orld in his hands," and he stops, begins to sing along with me, face wrapped in the T-shirt, arms stuck up like bound branches. "He's got you and me brother, in his hands." I'm tempted to just rip it off him, but I reach up and begin to untangle the shirt, setting him free.

He tosses the shirt at Teddy Bear and I figure it's best to just grab him a new one. I begin unbuttoning his PJs.

"Beautiful Teddy Bear," he says, calming himself. "You're not the enemy."

"Teddy Bear's a good friend," I say.

"He's got Teddy Bear in his hands," George sings.

He reaches his arms in the air to help me dress him. I won't say it didn't take some getting used to, dressing and undressing a man. But everything about this home is different than the way I lived before, and so all of these things have stopped feeling strange.

I pull the shirt over his arms and his head pops through. He looks deeply into my eyes, his arms still outstretched above him.

You really are a good-looking dude, I think. Anita tells him all the time, "Oh, George, you look so dapper! You'll turn all the girls' heads." And he smiles and says, "I am beautiful."

My brother Brian would be the same age as George now. About the same height too. But unlike George, Brian was able to finish high school, go to a great university and pursue his PHD. in philosophy. Unlike George, Brian was well, or so we thought until he sent me an email at the end of term telling me how I was going to do wonderful things to make this world a better place. While I was wondering what brought on his sudden sappiness, his roommate and best friend found him hanging from the doorway with an extension cord around his neck, a Post-it note on his chest that said, I'M SO SORRY—SO SORRY TO DO THIS TO YOU. PLEASE DON'T HATE ME. I JUST HAD NOTHING LEFT TO GIVE.

It was deemed a "depression-related accident" because we were all baptized Catholic and we needed to have the funeral in the Catholic Church, and the word *suicide* doesn't go over well with them. I was in second year and my professors let me postpone my exams, so I came home for the summer to do nothing but sleep and eat. My parents became so concerned about me that they sat me down and offered to pay my way to Europe if I would agree to stay at a Catholic retreat centre in France. We had never been a very pious family, but it seems that, in times of tragedy, we dig into our roots as some sort of grounding.

The retreat centre was covered in vegetable gardens and trees and had hundreds of places to sit with your thoughts and everyone was kind. You couldn't walk past a person without getting a smile. We were all assigned chores around the grounds and gathered for meals. We gathered in the mornings and evenings for candlelit services where we sang chants—beautiful, simple chants. *By night we hasten in darkness to search for the living water. Only our thirst leads us onward.* Chants that made me feel for once that I might be able to carry a tune, that allowed me to shut down my thoughts and be present and yet tuned out. *Come and fill our hearts with your peace.* Chants that let me join with whatever cosmic force was out there, join the people gathered around, enter into something that didn't have words.

But they were rigid about wake-up times and attending meals and showing up for your chores and I grew tired of structure and ritual. Or maybe it was the weight of the kindness and having too much time to think while gardening and walking through the hilly grounds. Either way, after two weeks of being woken up by an incessant bell at six-thirty in the morning, I took off to backpack France and Spain.

Everywhere I went I kept humming or singing those chants, down dirt roads and in old cathedrals. I found myself drawn to old pilgrimage trails. I'd step onto them for a few miles or a few dozen, meet others on the journey, stop at small churches and sit. If there was no one else there I'd sing, "Only our thirst leads us onward." Sometimes I'd sing even if someone was there, and sometimes a voice would join mine. It seemed that at every hostel I stayed at, every bar I stopped at, I'd run into someone who had visited the retreat centre. And I'd want to sing the chants with them, to see if they knew the same songs, to feel the comfort of someone else's voice joining mine. It happened again and again, to the point where I felt I must be missing out on something, and that something might be awful or it might be wonderful—there was no way to know in advance. But there was only so long I could miss it for.

So I returned to the retreat in late summer and stayed into the fall, ran into the academic year with no desire to finish my degree. I worked the gardens and did whatever heavy lifting was needed around the property, memorized songs and prayers, made friends with people who were passing through, and was happy with the transience of my relationships. After we harvested the vegetables I ran out of my parents' money and realized I needed to see them again. I came home to find they had split up. I had no way of knowing whether that's what they had in mind when they sent me away in the first place.

I decided to visit Maison de la Paix. I'd heard about it over the years, Christmastime offerings at Mass and things like that. Something about my trip to Europe had made me unafraid of approaching new people, so I biked over to the address by the ravine and rang the doorbell.

A man with Down syndrome opened the door. "Welcome to Paix," he said. "How can we welcome you?"

I had come to see if they had any volunteer needs, but found myself saying instead, "Do you have any room for a newcomer?"

"We always welcome newcomers," he said then called for Anita.

Anita told me they usually asked participants to volunteer for a month before moving into the community. "But I have a good feeling about you," she said. It might have had something to do with the fact that they needed someone with muscles. Whatever the reason, I moved in the next day and have been living here for three years.

Now when I tell people what I do, they commend me for "giving back," as if what I do isn't for me but for the people I live with, and as if I had anything to give to begin with. When people consider the diaper changes and restraining holds and lifting people who can't walk and hanging out with people who can't talk, they say, "I could never do that," and I remember how I used to feel like that.

When George has washed his face and brushed his teeth, chewing the bristles for most of it, I ask, "What do you want to do today, George?"

"Walk the train tracks."

Walking the train tracks out behind the house has always felt like an excitingly risky game with George. Despite his love of the hulking machines, his constant insistence on wearing his conductor's hat (sometimes with nothing else on), he's afraid of them in the steel, when they're moving. Once we took the group for an outing to take a train ride—one of those little things that run in a circle around the other rides at the midway. We thought he would be thrilled and he was for the three days leading up to it. "Going to take the train!" we could hear him yell to himself over and over while trying to fall asleep the night before.

When he saw the train, he lost his shit, screaming, "Train! Train!" and we were pretty thrilled about how happy he was, until we realized there was fear behind his eyes. He jumped up and down on the spot fifty feet away and wouldn't go any closer. I stayed with him trying to help him de-escalate while the others moved on to some of the other rides. His screams slowly subsided into whispers and finally I was able to guide him back to the parking lot. We spent the afternoon at a sticky picnic table eating soft-serve ice cream.

Still I take him out often to walk the tracks that run behind our house and into town. The train only runs on Friday afternoons and it's a quiet walk beside the ravine. We walk silently in each other's company, our backs to the sun.

It was Sonya who first suggested we start walking here with George. Sonya started volunteering with Paix about a year after I moved in. She would swing by after work and help make meals once a week.

It's easy to fall in love here, in a place where life is slower, where people look each other in the eyes, where kindness is taught and sung and prayed. Sonya started staying late into the evenings, brought her guitar and took requests as we sang together in the living room. Then she would stay on as people were tucking in, and she and I would walk at dusk along the tracks behind the house, make out in the dewy grass along the ravine. She had a beautiful way of articulating the things I had been feeling about Paix. "It's amazing," she said, "the way you see things differently when surrounded by people who don't define you by what you produce." "There are so few places in the world where people can just be." I liked that Sonya didn't know about Brian, didn't need to know, and yet I knew that whenever I chose to tell her she would listen and learn to love him without ever meeting him.

She was particularly close to Adam, the sweet man with Down's, and Patricia who couldn't speak but would communicate by pointing to words on a mat on her wheelchair. But as I was closest to George, I wanted her to get to know him better. She had always been friendly with George, but kept her distance. She's slight and gentle, and she knew he was unpredictable.

Once during one of our walks I vented about an argument I'd had with another staff member who wanted to encourage the doctors to give George something to make him calmer.

"I agree with her," she said. "They need to look at stronger medication, for George's sake."

"You can't be serious," I said. "You think he should walk around like a zombie?"

"Of course not! I take anti-anxiety meds, and I hope you don't think I'm a zombie."

"He's already on anti-anxiety pills! You don't know how bad these anti-psychotic meds are, the kind of long-term damage they do. I don't think it's fair for us to put George through that for our own comfort."

"Nobody benefits from him flying off the handle, especially not him."

"You should see him when he's drugged up—just a shell of himself."

"You need to give people time to adjust to their meds. It takes months sometimes."

"You can't just hang around the people who are easy to be with!"

She looked away, hurt.

"I'm sorry," I said. "I just think you think he's worse than he is," I said.

"Maybe," she said. "Maybe I just need to spend a little more time with him."

"I would love that," I said.

So we began walking together, the three of us, after supper along the tracks. It went well for the first few weeks, Sonya in the middle, holding both of our hands. But one day a stray mutt came running towards us and George flipped out.

"Enemy!" George yelled. He began thrashing and smacked Sonya across the face.

"George!" she said sternly. He turned to her with an expression that suggested she had set the dog on him and reached for her throat.

I pulled him off of her, pinned him in a standing restraint.

"It's alright, George. The dog is gone," I said, but he was livid with her.

"Fucking enemy!" he yelled at her.

She ran her hand along her red, raw neck.

"Are you alright?" I said, trying to speak in a calming voice as George bulked against my arms. I was about to say sorry, but I didn't want to apologize on George's behalf.

She looked at me as if I had been the one to hit her.

"You shouldn't have put me in this situation," she said, barely audible over George's yells.

"I'm sorry you got hurt," I said. "But these things happen. It's part of getting to know him."

"He's violent and he obviously doesn't want to be!"

"You're stigmatizing him."

"You don't get it—you're bigger than him!"

I felt angry holding George still and talking about him as if he weren't there.

"He needs to be better medicated!" she yelled.

"Fucking medicine!" George yelled.

"George, it's okay," I said. "Sonya, you'd better go. He won't calm down while you're around. He feels too badly about it."

"At least someone does," she said as she turned to leave.

SHE CALLED ME the next evening. "I'm sorry," she said. "I would have done this in person, but it's just too hard to see everyone."

"I'm really sorry about what happened," I said, though I was still angry with her reaction.

"Thanks," she said, "but I just don't feel like this is going to work out. Please say bye to Adam and Patricia for me."

"Not George?" I said hotly.

"I wouldn't want to upset him."

My anger made it easier to deal with missing her. She was right; I was bigger than him. But many other people on staff were not and they could handle him just fine.

George climbs the slight incline up to the tracks. He crouches down and sits on one side of the iron rail, picks a tiny buttercup growing inside a wooden tie. I sit down across from him on the other rusty rail. He reaches his long arm towards me and places it on my head.

"God made you beautiful," he says to the buttercup.

"Thank you," I say.

"He's got the whole world in his hands," he sings softly. I sing along.

"Yikes! Thunder," George says.

"Really, George? I don't hear it." I feel it before I see it, the tracks quivering slightly beneath us.

"Yikes!" George says again as the rumble grows stronger. He pulls into himself, arms wrapped tightly around himself.

"Okay, George," I say calmly, looking up to see the spot

of the dark train growing towards us. "We're going to go sit in the grass and watch the train go by."

I realize my mistake as soon as I say it.

"Train!" he says wildly from within his arms. He wraps them more tightly, presses himself down against the track. The whistle blows.

"Fucking enemy!" he yells.

"Come on, George. We've got to move."

George holds firm to his place. I grab for his arm. He swats me away.

"Come on," I say firmly, leaning over him and trying to pull him up to stand. George has curled into a ball, his arms wrapped tightly around his legs so I can't drag him by the chest. Finally he has learned how to beat the restraints I've been taught.

I try to push him gently by the shoulders but he won't budge. The whistle blows wildly. He begins to thrash at me with his fists. His fist lands in my eye and I pull back. I put my hand to my throbbing face.

"Damn it, George! Get off the fucking tracks!" I hear the train's brakes squealing but it is still reeling towards us. My eye burns and begins to run.

I stand over the rumbling tracks. I dare not look at the train, but sense the wind of it approaching. I push hard against his knees. He screams as he tumbles backwards down the grassy incline and I roll after him.

When I reach him I crouch over his sprawled body to put him in a hold. The train rolls by, still whistling vehemently. He reaches up from the ground and punches me again, same eye as before.

I punch him in the stomach. George wails and pulls into himself.

I stand in front of him.

George is huddled on the ground, hands on his stomach, winded. He looks up at me like a dog that's been kicked.

I move my mouth to say, "I'm sorry," but I can't, even though I feel like shit. It's possible to be drenched in guilt and still not be sorry.

"You're the enemy!" says George breathlessly into the grass beneath us. He lifts a fist to punch the air at me then flinches away.

"I fucking saved you!" I yell back. I say it over again in my head, convincing myself.

"You fucking saved me," he says back, as if it hurts him to say.

I reach in the emergency pack over my shoulder and pull out George's tranquilizer pills. I pop the blister pack, pass him a water bottle, take his palm and place the pill in it. "Please take this," I say.

"You tried to kill me!" he yells and throws the pill at the tracks.

"George, you know that's not true," I say, but I'm not sure if he does. "You know I want to take care of you." I grab another pill and take his hand again. I'll have to find the pill later or fill out the paperwork to account for it. His long fingernails dig into my palm. My eyebrow starts to throb. I wonder how I will account for his bruises, how I will tell my boss that I punched him, if I'll be fired, and where else I would go if I couldn't be at Paix.

"Look at me," I say. He looks into my eyes. "Please take this. It will make you feel better."

He looks back at me with a look I can't interpret. You mean it will make *you* feel better, I imagine him saying.

He puts the pill on his tongue and takes a swig of water, then another, then gulps back the whole bottle. He crushes the flimsy plastic in his fist.

He lies back in the grass and I wait for the drugged smile to creep across his lips. "You know I love you want to take care of you," he says into the clouds.

"I know," I say.

"You know I've got the whole world in my hands," he says. "The whole beautiful world in my hands."

ACKNOWLEDGEMENTS

Many of these stories are set in a fictional town inspired by the beautiful community in which I grew up. While the landscape and atmosphere inspired the setting, all stories and characters are fictional.

Great thanks to the literary journals that published earlier versions of these stories: *The Puritan*, *Grain*, *Joyland*, *Paragon*, *Ryga*, *Joypuke*, *A Common Thread*, and *Here Be Monsters*.

Thank you to Hugh Cook, who first guided me through the short story writing process; to Katherine Govier for the feedback, hospitality, and kindness; to Michael Winter for helping me find details that spark in a story; to Rosemary Sullivan for wisdom and inspiration.

Many thanks to my creative writing program workshop buddies: Laura Hartenberger, Susannah Showler, Phoebe Wang, Molly Lynch, Andres Vatiliotou, and Jennifer Last, as well as Andrew Sullivan, Brendan Bowles, and Catriona Wright. Special thanks to Sharon Helleman and Laura Hartenberger for her support and for creating a lovely atmosphere in which to write from home.

Thank you to Taryn Boyd for being such a wonderful support and companion in making *The Whole Beautiful World* a reality, to Colin Thomas for exceptional insight and warm encouragement, to Tree Abraham for the cover design, to Pete Kohut for the interior design, to Kate Kennedy for copyediting, to Renée Layberry for all the editing support, and to Tori Elliott for getting the word out. Thanks, Brindle & Glass, for making the creation of this book such a great experience.

Much love to Peter Norman and Melanie Little for helping me through the bookmaking process.

Thank you to countless friends and family who have read these stories and offered your thoughts and inspiration in the writing process.

Thank you, Dad, for your unending love and interest in everything I do; and eternal thanks to Mom—though you are not here to read my words, I think of you with every story I write.

To Elliott, for allowing me a little time during your new life to do revisions. Finally, thank you, Mark Norman, my sounding board, my best friend, my love.